T0193563

The
Magenta
Door

The Magenta Door

RAYMOND C. WOOD

THE MAGENTA DOOR

iUniverse books may be ordered through booksellers or by contacting:

iUniverse
1663 Liberty Drive
Bloomington, IN 47403
www.iuniverse.com
1-800-Authors (1-800-288-4677)

ISBN: 978-1-5320-3361-2 (sc)
ISBN: 978-1-5320-3360-5 (e)

Library of Congress Control Number: 2017915034

Print information available on the last page.

iUniverse rev. date: 12/04/2017

Preface

In all accounts Amy Rudy was a loving and faithful wife to her husband Josh and was totally flabbergasted when her employer left her $100,000 their "Will" but she was extremely put out by her coworkers $350,000 payout. In her way of thinking he was just a single retired plumber who gets a juicy pension.

So with the help of a young lawyer whom she seduces and a disbarred lawyer who she "bribes big time "they changed the" Will". However when the plumber finds out an ungodly rage threatens to take all of them down!

Dedicated to Dave Richard my best friend who pulled me off that bridge so many, long, long years ago. Rest in peace-1/30/45-7/18/2017

Chapter 1

J osh Rudy emerged from the garage at his house, satisfied that once again it was another mechanical victory in changing the oil on his older Dodge ram truck. Changing the oil is something he picked up from his father ever since he bought his first car. As he closed the garage door he looked around and reflected on the cozy house that was silhouetted in the crisp air, sounded by evergreen trees. To the side sat an old oak tree that must have been spared by the developers, stood like a giant centenarian soldier on a half-acre of mostly green lawn. A tree line in was in the back as a boundary with a couple of stunted holly bushes on the other side.

He and his loving wife, Amy of 11 years had kind of hit the jackpot when they found the small two-bedroom ranch with attached garage on the market at a price they could afford. Pooling their monies each before they tied the knot.

She was due at any time from work. Under her instructions he had prepared the small roast for the evening meal, hoping he did it right. Amy was one hell of a cook; she was one of six Irish kids in a family that loved all the gaiety and family bonding at the evening meal. He could hear the Chevy in the distance. Its muffler was spewing and huffing, and Josh knew that they somehow must find the money to replace it. Moving to their new digs they barley scraped by because of his spotty hours working for a stonemason. However, they sort of had a pack that in either thick or thin they like many young people buying their first home they would somehow prevail.

Amy drove down the short driveway pulling up smiling as he opened the door for her, quipping "Well what do know it's my old high school sweetheart. Are you lost lass'?

'Very funny honey. You keeping an eye on the roast"?

"Yeah it's in the oven almost ready."

Even though they been married almost a dozen years, he loved to eyeball her lovely features. Today her short skirt and calico blouse that was tailor made, was enhancing her flowing brown hair, smooth congenial face, and eyes that seemed always glowing and warm. A great shape she had, that hours in the cellar with a bevy of gym equipment gave her that well defined tone. At only 29 she was his little cutie pie.

"Come on Josh, lets tend to the roast, if you followed my directions it should be fine."

Inside she removed it from the oven rack, saying, "It looks like we're ready to eat."

Josh breathed a sigh of relief. He hated doing these tasks in the kitchen. Of course, he would never tell her that, because she would want to cook every night, sometimes exhausted from work. Getting take out too often proved to be an added expense.

He already set the table and Amy quickly warmed up the vegetables and spuds. He cracked open a bottle of champagne. For any big meal, out came the bubbly stuff.

The only downside was it always made him sleepy and sometimes put the brakes on his ideas that would like to transpire in the bedroom.

"So, what's new in Bensonville?" He asked as he downed more champagne.

Amy took a light sip and said, "Not too much hon, although my boss seems to be happy the way I've been putting and cataloging the merchandise in the computer for sale."

"That's great." Josh beamed, "Maybe a raise is in order?"

Amy got up stirring the potatoes and vegetables she prepared yesterday. "Well, I can't say too much since I've only been working there a little over a year. I am just glad I took computer classes right after high school."

"Yeah, that was a good move," as he stood up wrapping his arms around her neck, "How come I am so lucky to get both a good looking broad, and a great cook"?

"Honey" she looked up suspiciously, "Every time you drink that stuff you hug me and I can feel your bulge pressing against me," then she giggled, "then like the champagne when it loses it fizz it comes crashing down."

Kind of embarrassed he sat back down saying, "I should have a beer."

"Come on Josh, you know we both love champagne at meals like roasts. You my husband drink too fast, and sometimes half the bottle."

Josh sighed and agreed with her without saying a word.

"Don't worry sexy" as she perused his rugged good looks smiling, "There's plenty of time for other things."

After she cut the meat and loaded his plate up, while fixing hers she says, "Your boss gives you Saturday off now?"

"The truth of it?" Josh replied, "He wants to cut back, so that means the other two masons and lumpers like me don't work Saturdays." "Oh, Josh," Amy looked at him seriously, "I really kind of wish you get into another line of work. Not so much of cutting back hours, but I worry about you killing yourself lifting those rocks, coming home totally spent. Lord, you're already built like man mountain dean!"

"I know honey but the money is good even though it's not union. Plus, when we go to Cape Cod and sometimes up to Boston, he pays lodging and gas expenditures. Besides, not only are you working for Rodgers and Rodgers five days a week, until recently you would go up to NorthPark to work at the store."

Then Josh thought, "The only thing honey, is that with the Saturday pay I was going to replace the skins on the pickup."

"What shame Josh," Amy sadly said, "that your Uncle Bert's tire shop burnt down, what was it five years now?"

"Yeah, he always gave me a cut on the price, but it is what it is."

Chapter 2

Meanwhile in the small hamlet of NorthPark, Mrs. Viola Rego was trying to hold on to the store that she and her husband Al had started some forty plus years ago. It has been 17 months since Al fell down the stairs in the stores cellar and died from massive head trauma.

The police said somehow, he tripped hitting his head on the cellar floor. An autopsy revealed what she already knew. At seventy-five, he was in top shape, no issues like medication or drinking. But she couldn't understand. He went down those stairs at least twice a day to get light supplies, it just didn't add up. Al could have retired a hundred times, but he loved the smiles on the kids coming in buying penny candy, and the camaraderie with all his friends that were regular customers who have supported them. Then she reflected thinking we never made any money on penny candy, not even a penny, but that was something he wanted to continue from the day they opened.

It has been hard since Al's passing. She had to let go of Mike, a part-timer who loved to help and did any repairs. Then, of course there is Amy Rudy from over in Mt Granite who also worked part time, marrying a local of NorthPark.

So, after being closed for a considerable amount of time

she decided to re-open. Also, her desire to be moving around at 68 years old, she felt it was something Al would have wanted her to do.

Their home, a small cottage, was on the same locale. A hop, skip and jump from the store.

Chapter 3

Around six months later, on a Monday morning, there was a blustery raw wind that came from the Northeast as Josh backed the pickup from the garage. He was heading to NorthPark where his next job was. He was debating on whether to stop in to see Mrs. Rego after work, since he was in town and grew up in area, and was in the store tons of time when he was a kid. Also, the fact he hasn't been there since Amy started working again in the last few months. He always remembered coming into the store and joking with Al. He always had a yarn or two, and making fun of the no-good politicians. In fact, his best friend growing up worked for Al during high school.

But after working on a wall at a local selectman's stately eighteenth-century mansion, Josh was kind of be beat, so for now he would skip the visit. For some reason though, he wanted to see the stairs where Al fell. Thinking though, he knew would be unwise to bring that up while Mrs. Rego was there. He would wait sometime when only Amy was there, probably when Mrs. Rego went to church Sunday mornings. Amy told him that for some reason Mrs. Rego still can't wrap her head around why Al just suddenly tripped down the stairs for apparently no good reason. So, after work he drove by the store called Al's then headed home to Mount Granite joining Amy who was already there.

She had put together some meat pies in the oven," Hey champ!" she greeted him as he came in, placing a peck on the cheek.

Josh twisted around, acting silly, making confuted facial expressions and began a half- hearten effort to act sillier as he said, 'Hey baby it's the Big Bopper speaking," then went into," ooheeooh-oohahn-walla walla a binge bang" grabbing, the salt shaker as a mike.

"Josh," Amy interjected," Not even close! Two different songs my crazy husband."

"Now why don't you jump in the shower before the pies get done."

Josh's mood suddenly went from being a poor comedian, to a hungry stomach growling imbecile as his smell senses took over. " Be back in a jiffy" as he rattled, "See you later alligator!" then went to the bathroom.

Amy yelled out, "Not too long."

On his quick return Amy said, "You look human with all that rock dust gone."

"Yeah, and I feel just as good." Josh replied. "So," he said as Amy handed him a beer, "When do you work at the store again?"

"Sunday for a few hours in the morning."

"Goo.," he smiled as he chugged down the beer. "I had a feeling it was this Sunday."

"Why, what's up?"

"Honey I would love to see the stair case where Al fell, before Mrs. Rego gets back from church."

"Why Josh?"

"Well, going on what you've been telling me, how she doesn't know for sure what made Al fall, the autopsy revealing nothing; where was she when Al fell?"

"My understanding," Amy said as she removed the two pies from the oven, "She was in the front of the store waiting on a mom and her two toddlers."

"What did the cops conclude?" Josh asked digging into the tasty pie.

"What are you suddenly Sherlock Homes?" Amy laughed as she poured herself a glass of milk. Josh grinned, "Not really, it's more of a curiosity then anything."

"OK Dick Tracy, be at the store between 9 and 10."

Josh adjusted his belt saying, "Was Mrs. Rego sure that nobody was around when it happened?"

"What are you driving at my sleuth?"

Josh could see the doubts in her eyes almost if it were a sign spelling the words out. Josh leaned back in his chair cupping his chin, "Well I don't know hon, I am playing detective."

Amy collected the dirty dishes and deposited them in the dishwasher, bending over in her endeavor. Josh grinned and feasted on her butt knowing she was wearing those so-called yoga pants. She caught his glaze, spinning completely around. "What are you staring at, my over sexed husband?"

"Sorry baby." He got up from the chair grabbing her backside.

"Josh leave my ass alone, I am trying to load the dishwasher." Her voice cracking a bit with laughter. "Oh, are you now?" as he again grabbed her.

She playfully broke away running into the living room, Josh his mouth wide open yelling, "I'm going to get you," grabbing her around the waist. "Ha-ha the big bad wolf has got you now, and I am going to take off your pants!" "Oh no you don't," she half heartily tried to stop him until he threw a lip lock and reached for her waistband. When suddenly they heard a knock on the door.

Chapter 4

"**D**amn," Josh mumbled, "Who could that be?" Amy wiping her brow said, "Find out while I fix my clothes!"

Josh reluctantly tried to compose himself as he opened the door.

"Oh, hi Becky."

She notated his face looked flush smiling, "I hope I didn't interrupt anything?"

"Oh, no, no hon your sister is here," he exclaimed loud enough for Amy to hear.

Amy walked over, "Becky, how are you? What a nice surprise."

Becky was Amy's older sister, and married to a trucker Pedro Lopez, a rather contentious marriage to be sure Josh thought. She was a little taller than Amy, with shoulder length hair. She was in a power suit so they knew she just came from work.

"Coffee on?" Becky asked.

"It will be now," Amy responded, "Last time we talked on the phone you were telling that your car was acting up."

Becky grabbed a seat saying, "Yeah, the battery was giving me trouble until Pedro went to a salvage yard and replaced it. Nothing so damn lame as worrying if your car is going to start."

"So how do we process the honor of your company?" Josh smiled as he got three cups.

Becky had a half grin, adjusting her blouse as it was riding down showing more cleavage. Amy knew that the new thing now with women is showing more, and Josh must be taking it all in.

"So big sister, something must be up for you to come from work."

"Of course," Becky agreed, aware of Josh eying her. "You guys of course know that Pedro's cousin is a Lieutenant with the NorthPark P.D., well I thought you should know especially Amy, that Mrs. Rego has a $1,000,000-dollar life insurance on her husband. Double indemnity clause in case of one or both should die from an accidental death."

Josh standing against a wall said, "Wow that's a bit unusual, for a double indemnity I would think."

"Well," Becky further said, "My understanding, since no foul play was found, that the preponderance of evidence was dismissed."

Then she glanced at Josh kind of nervous that Amy would notice her husband ogling her tits.

"So, what does that mean?" Amy questioned.

"It means, that in the evidence ascertained by the detectives and the insurance company, Al wasn't pushed by someone. That would of course mean murder but a few people think otherwise."

"So," Josh said, "How do know so much about it?"

"Pedro knows most of the cops and was told about the investigation," Becky said as Josh poured the fresh coffee.

Sipping her coffee Becky then opted to take the building drama out of the conservation, "I think it was a way of a loving wife to have a fall back in case of a tragedy."

Amy got up from the table saying, "I am kind of mystified that suddenly there are questions to do with money about Al falling, it's almost like the cops are saying there's a sinister motive here."

"No," Becky voiced, "I don't think the cops are saying Mrs. Rego had anything to do with her husband falling."

"I hope not," Amy got a little perturbed, "Mrs. Rego adored her husband, they were soul mates."

Josh putting his thoughts into words," Don't worry honey, I don't think the cops think she pushed Al down the stairs. In a small town like NorthPark where there is hardly anything going on rumors kind of get traction."

"Well," Becky said as she finished her coffee, "I must get back, Pedro will be looking for his grub. Don't worry I'll keep you guys informed of any new information."

Amy still uptight said, "Even the slightest thought that Al was pushed down the stairs would be too much for her, she's frail enough."

"Oh, don't worry." Becky responded walking out, and getting into her late model Lexus, "It's all on the Q.T."

Josh admiring her car said, "Nice ride, when did you get this?"

"A couple months ago, Pedro bought it for me. He also bought me a new battery, but after much wrangling the dealer reimbursed him."

"Well they should, hell it's almost new."

A gusty wind blew with an icy chill as the Lexus throaty

sound could be heard throughout the quiet neighborhood. Josh could see that Amy was still upset, "Are you OK babes?"

"I don't know Josh, I just hope that these rumors don't get back to Mrs. Rego."

Josh thought for a second, "Now I am wondering, maybe it wouldn't be a good idea, me snooping around after this disclosure."

"Don't be ridiculous" Amy sternly responded, "A husband can visit his wife, can't he?"

"You're right," Josh gleaned, "I'll be there around 10 Sunday".

Chapter 5

Leo Rego was on his way to the store in NorthPark, Mass. from nearby Rhode Island. A forty-five-year-old, successful used furniture dealer who always made money no matter what businesses he had been in over the years, and Viola Rego's only son, said he would be stopping in around 3 PM.

Amy arrived early in the morning so Viola could attend church, then she would open the store. Amy walked in smiling.

"Amy, I can always tell by your car you are here."

"I know Viola the muffler is really getting bad. So how are you doing?"

Viola a short stoutly woman, with a crisscross of lines that lightly masked her face, bore the advancing of age and probably the sudden stress about her husband.

"Oh, I am fine I suppose under the circumstances. But on a high note my son Leo is on his way around 3, you must have met him a few times?"

"Oh yes," Amy was quick to point out, "and at the services."

"Of course," Viola suddenly remembered. "Well, Mrs. Chaves is going to pick me up soon. Would you mind cleaning up around the detergents? One of them leaked and you might as well straighten the area up."

"No problem," Amy reiterated, "When did you say your son was coming?"

"He said around three or four after he drops off a load of furniture near Boston."

About a half hour after Viola left, Amy heard someone rummaging around a storage room near the cellar. Amy cautiously went to investigate but then stopped and composed herself thinking who would be there? For sure the customers don't go in there. Then suddenly the door opened and a small peaked man stepped in whom she instantly recognized, it was her former coworker Mike Fremont.

"Oh, hi Amy I was fetching my tool kit that I forgot when she closed the store. I hope I didn't startle you?"

"Of course not," Amy smiled, "Good to see you Mike, I remembered you did all the repairs."

"Yeah that I did, working part time for Al almost 11 years."

Amy studied the retiree, probably around 69-70, although he was small in stature he was as strong as an ox and she remembered he was a plumber by trade.

"So, you're working again Amy?"

"Just a few hours, mostly on Sunday so Viola can go to church."

"That's great," Mike said in a pleasant response, "I feel better already that someone is helping her."

Amy turned to the front of the store, "Looks like a customer."

Mike in his hoarse crackling voice said, "OK Amy, I'll stop by some Sunday when I have more time."

With that Amy went to wait on the customer. Within twenty minutes Josh pulled up. While walking in Josh asked, "Any business?"

"Just a few people, and I saw Mike Fremont."

"Oh ya, I remember Mike he was a fixture here, although I only met him once or twice." Then Josh laughed, "I guess I'll play Sherlock now."

Amy went with him to the cellar stairs and opened the door. Josh flipped the light switch on "It's not too steep of a staircase, but I suppose at his age falling it could have been just a few steps."

"I agree" Amy sadly said.

Josh put his hand to his three-day whiskers "I wonder if the cops checked his shoe's? I wonder if those were the ones he always wore, or if he bought new ones and they were slippery."

"Come on darling, this may be a small town but the cops I am sure checked out that theory."

Josh looking at the brightly colored cellar door said. "So, that's why they obviously call it the magenta door to the cellar."

"Yes," Amy said, "Viola told me the family they bought the store from, the Gustafson's, who had three kids, gave the kids a bucket of magenta paint he found somewhere and told them to paint the wall at the bottom of the staircase, to keep them focused after school when they were a handful. Viola then said they would call it the magenta cellar because of a side entrance with a cellar door outside, but after a while the kids painted the door, so the name stuck, and unfortunately it was later where Al died opening the magenta door.

"Oh, a customer," Amy perked up, "Now don't be too long, Viola will be here in about 20 minutes OK?"

"Got that." Josh answered.

When the customer left, Josh went up front, "Well Amy girl, Sherlock Holmes I am not, so I better get going."

Chapter 6

Attorney Jack Cohen was on his way to the store. He was a middle aged, married man who was Viola's attorney, and was very forward whenever he was in her company. Amy disliked him immensely, but kept her cool because of Viola.

His son River on other hand, was just the opposite, probably because he was his stepson. He had called when Josh left saying he was coming to see Viola. Amy tried to delay him until Viola returned, but she knew he wanted to do what he always does; flirt like he's God's gift to women.

The black Lincoln pulled up and Amy braced herself. Jack Cohen walked in saying,

"Well Amy, good to see you again. You look like you have been working."

"Well ya, I suppose that's why I am here, to work," Amy tersely responded.

Jack ignored her comment, "So how is your husband?"

"He's fine." Amy thought he was probably hoping that they broke up or something.

Then he started checking her out, especially her yoga pants. His eyes then were trained on her breasts, that were straining against the halter top she wore. Then he commented in a drool, "The maker did well when he made you."

Amy wanted so bad to tell him to fuck off, but was saved when Mrs. Chaves pulled up in her old attention getting 53' Dodge Coronet station wagon. Without saying anything, she went to help Viola into the store. Viola smiled, "Thanks honey, I am not crippled yet, but thank you."

Then, she noticed the Black Lincoln. "Oh, I see that Jack's here."

Around seven PM, Amy was on her way home. Thankfully, she had busied herself with customers as Jack and Viola went into the office. Driving home, she was thinking--she knew that Josh and herself worked hard for whatever they had, but now it seems like they would never get ahead. The Chevy drove up and Josh opened the door for her.

"Honey, you look peaked, you must have "turned too" at the store."

"That I did, but it was also because of Viola's obnoxious attorney, Jack Cohen who visited her."

"I remember him, you paint a good description of that louse."

Of course, Amy would leave out the part of him always trying to get her underneath the bed sheets. Josh would snap him like a pretzel! Then Amy went on, "After asshole left, her son Leo came over and I was in the back room tiding up when I heard them arguing, and it wasn't what I would call very friendly."

"What were they arguing about?"

"Couldn't hear, but" Amy looking puzzled continued,

"Now why would anybody yell at Viola, notwithstanding his own mother?"

"Beats me." Josh shrugged it off, "It could be anything." "Say baby I got a great idea, why don't we fill the tub up, I've got a couple of joints. We can just relax, we haven't done that in a while."

Amy gave an agreeable smirk. Josh could already see himself painting her body with his tongue.

Chapter 7

As they wallowed in the warm bath water facing each other, Amy took a deep drag harmonizing with the music from the radio then saying, "Hon pass me the bar of Caress."

In a minute or so she passed the joint to Josh who leaned inward kissing her breasts. She kind of pushed him away, "Not now lover boy, wait until we get out and into our bed."

"Well OK, if I can stand it that long."

"Relax baby, we got all night."

But when Josh leaned back in the shallow water, Amy's mouth dropped as his cock with a full erection emerged from under the suds.

Josh knew that sometimes, smoking pot relaxed him so much that only a small window was open before it decided to go from attention, to at ease. Amy suddenly lurched forward grabbing all of his genitalia, "Honey," she rubbed his balls, "You know that you're holding, in your lovely jewelry bag, sperm that I want into my chamber. I want a baby!"

Josh was shocked, "You always said you wanted to wait."

"I know my handsome husband, but at 29 it's time. Wouldn't you think?"

Josh exclaimed with a mile-long sexy grin, "I'm roaring, and ready to go into the bed."

"Relax champ, lets enjoy the moment, but not for too long. Already my little pussy is hyperventilating waiting for your arrival."

After several more hits on the so called funny stuff, they went in the bedroom. Josh experienced everything, he seemed to be abstract. He felt in his mind he had boarded a jet plane and Amy was on a Caribbean island waiting for him in a loving embrace.

"Josh!" Amy shouted to him, but still he was on a floating dream where colorful candy canes and a tapestry of brilliant colors painted the sky.

"Josh, where did you get this stuff?," she exclaimed, then grabbing his semi hard manhood.

Then she did everything in her arsenal to keep him aroused, but Josh was still in that ginger bread house somewhere North of Dallas. Finally, she covered him up, and got next to his limp body thinking there's one thing for sure, no baby tonight!

Josh stirred when Amy called him. Glancing at the clock he was shocked it was in the AM.

"I made coffee my falling Knight of Amour."

Then Josh remembered the wacky weed sent him to another dimension. Amy gave him a quick look, "Hon, I am running late, see you tonight." As she leaned over to kiss him, Josh pulled her into him and she could feel his cock on the rebound, "Honey it's too late, I've got to go!"

"OK, sorry about last night I ah,"

"Never mind," she cut him off squeezing his throbbing cock, "I want this tonight."

Chapter 8

Josh got home kind of early. After considerable time, he called Amy's cell and she said she was doing some catch up with the files. After about a month of different excuses; working late, shopping, checking out a sale, so on and so forth, and then in the bedroom she could hardly keep her eyes open. Saturday rolled around and Amy was ready to go to the store in NorthPark. Josh looked over disappointed and Amy picked it up.

"Oh Josh, I know I haven't been too accommodating lately, it's just I've been busy at work and other things."

Josh reminded her, "Honey, you're the one that told me you wanted a baby yet we hardly have sex anymore."

"Get ready darling when I come home," she said as she grabbed his crotch.

Josh started thinking about having a baby, and went to the reefer grabbing the milk then the Raisin Brand and dumping a ton of Wheat Germ on it. Thinking, "I hope it's a son, but a cute little doll of a daughter would be nice also."

At the store, Amy's cell phone jingled, and while Viola was waiting on a customer. Attorney Jack Cohen's stepson, River was out back of the store.

"River, why are you here now?" River grabbed her, "Sorry babe, I just had to be with you again."

"Easy," Amy pushed him away. "What did you find out?"

River, was slim, dark haired, attractive, around thirty-five, sported a thin goatee and was going to law school.

"I got into the files, but haven't had time to read it yet."

Amy concurred, "When are you able to find out more?"

"Soon." River said, clearly panting over her.

"I've got to get back inside."

"Wait!" River was almost in a panic, "When will I see you again?"

"Not too soon, my husband is complaining that I am always coming home late."

River's face came crashing down. Amy pinched his cheek, "Don't worry, you just get the information, and at some point, we will meet at the motel, and remember I'll call you. Don't call me."

"OK Amy." River was like a boy who suddenly had his new bike stolen under his nose.

Amy got home on time, and Josh decided to ramp up their pending Arabian night with candle's and a giant box of chocolates. Amy was overwhelmed saying, "Oh thee husband, what have you thou wrought?"

Josh was in a high-octane lust, as he knew now he would hopefully impregnate his lovey bride of 11 years.

Amy went into the bathroom, "You my horny husband, get in bed, give me a little time to freshen up."

Josh shed his clothes and fell into the bed contemplating their sexual extravaganza. Soon, Amy appeared in a revealing nighty that he got for her at Victoria Secret. "So," Amy

looked and smiled "What do I see sticking up in the sheet?"
"One guess," Josh laughed.

"Before we mate Tarzan, I never really asked you about your true thoughts of having a baby.

"Are you kidding babe? I would be so proud, that I would want to re root John Phillips Sousa from the grave to play his band."

Amy laughed, "Oh my God, Josh you're a piece of work."

"And you Amy girl, you're a piece of shining jewelry, that I still can't figure out how I got."

Amy looked down on his ballooning love tool.

"Come on now Amy, never mind lollygagging jump in bed!"

He quickly peeled off her nighty, planting kisses on her neck, then traveling down one side of her sweet body to her leg, then to her foot, massaging and blowing on it, then up the other side to the other foot. Amy just laid back, moaning in her aura. This time he moved in front of her, kissing and caressing her breasts, sucking her nipples. "Oh, Josh" she cried out. Then moving his tongue down, swirling around her belly so tight, so pronounced; then he entered her scintillating sanctuary with his finger.

"Josh! Yes, Josh!" Amy was paralyzed, in a long sexual fuse that seemed like a burning fire storm, as Josh then entered her with his throbbing cock, Up and down he thrust, and all Amy could do was to grab his buttocks in a volley of words and grunts that put her in a tizzy.

"Josh, oh God! Fuck me, fuck me hard!"

After twenty minutes or more, she down loaded her explosion, as Josh pulled his own trigger.

Then they caught their collective breaths, then she started half crying and half giggling.

"What's the matter Amy?" Josh was puzzled.

"Oh, nothing dear. I'm just so happy that I made you happy."

"Happy? That's a mild word, the way I feel. Hold on I've got to piss." Josh slid out of bed to the nearby bathroom, as Amy admired his muscular butt.

"Hey Tarzan, nice ass!"

Josh quickly rejoined her saying, "Maybe a baby huh? A baby for little Amy?"

But before she could react, he was down on her. Entering, and sliding his tongue into her.

"Oh my God Josh, what's gotten into you?"

But that was she would say for the next twenty-five minutes, as Josh licked, sucked, kissed and lapped. Twisting and swirling his tongue in her, then an ultimate flash inside her caused her to scream uncontrollably, it was like she lubed her genitalia with a dash of cocaine.

Finally, a star glazed Amy sat on the edge of the bed as Josh rubbed her back saying, "Maybe today might be where a baby might get his or her start;" "If not," Josh followed up, "We got the next day, and then the next day, plus the next."

Amy put her hand to her face, "Oh darling, your poor Amy wouldn't be able to walk for a week. Come on lover, let's get our clothes and take a ride into town, I want a frosty at Mel's.

Josh just laid there stroking his penis that was hard again.

"Are you sure Amy?"

Amy threw his pants at him, "Come, my Adonis."

"OK, OK." Josh quickly got dressed, "We'll take the pickup."

As Amy got in the truck, unbeknownst to Josh; she was now on the pill. No time for baby's in my new plans she thought.

Chapter 9

It was a glorious Saturday fall day, as they traversed though the neighborhood to the road into town. Josh was glad they both had the day off and finally could spend time together. As they got to town, Josh slowed down by Stokers Auto Body shop, and out front was a 71' Chevelle SS that the owner Jeff Newel was restoring. Amy could see in Josh's face that owning something like that was so remote.

"Don't worry honey, someday you might have your own toy."

All Josh said, was "Yeah right, on what planet?"

As they got more into town, a neighbor Rex Wainwright beeped and waved. Mount Granite was typical New England town, with the white church, and the pointed spirals. Stores of wood and brick and mortar, those few businesses that survived the huge discount bohemians on the edge of town. The usual couple of coffee shops trying to compete with the big donuts chains. One does so by having a bakery too. The town boasted of having an automotive school, and a clinic for fighting addiction abuse. Mount Granite was named because of an outcropping of a small, but deep Granite deposit on the edge of town, where there is a small park appropriately named Granite Park. A children's area, and a dog walk along with a few trails that people can enjoy.

It has been said that during revolutionary times, Mount Granite was infested with Tory's, but suffice to say most were driven out by the patriots fleeing to Canada. Even a few to England, and it was on record that most of the towns people burnt down the most prominent Tory house; a Colonel Andrews barely escaped with is life.

Josh grabbed Amy's hand, "Honey I love you."

She squeezed tightly saying, "I love you more."

The Dodge Ram pulled into Mel's. Josh said, "In or out?"

Amy had the door ajar, "Let's go in."

They took their seats, and Josh ordered two large frosty's, then gave Amy a penetrating laser beam smiling. Chuckling, he said, "Did you enjoy yourself earlier dear?"

Amy gave him a light kick under the table, "Honey, I'm so drained. I think I am going to need ten frosty's." They both laughed.

Amy commented, "They really have this place fixed up nice since the last time I was here."

As the waitress brought over their drinks, Amy in the corner of her eye, saw River's Suburban pull in the lot. Panicking, she was hoping he was going through the drive-up window, breathing a sigh of relief when that happened.

Josh saw her transfixed at the big window.

"What's up hon?"

"Oh, I was looking at how much businesses this place does."

Thinking though, she let River get caught up in her grand plan, and on a personal level that he could blow the whole thing, and Josh would tear him apart if he knew what he's done!

After spending the day doing many things, and visiting Amy's family in Bensonville, they headed back home to Mount Granite. Amy was decidability quiet on the way back, thinking about her master plan.

Josh commented, "Well, you will be going to the store in the morning I suppose," then he said "You have two jobs. and another month I'll be getting laid off for the winter. Yeah, hunky dory for me, in construction they call it *going down the road*." shrugging his shoulders.

"Don't worry hon, I got a feeling that things will be getting better for us in the future."

"Well," Josh breathed, "I'm glad you're an optimist."

Chapter 10

The next day, Amy drove to the store in NorthPark; thinking about what she has done and hoping her plan would work. Or would it spiral down in a ball of fire taking Josh with it?

Arriving at the store, and seeing Viola leave for church, Amy went into the office, remembering about a year before Al died, when Viola was at church.

Al was off resting on Viola's orders in their nearby home, and Viola asked her to tidy up the office. In that endeavor, she saw a set of keys on the floor, thinking that Viola probably dropped them, for she noticed she was getting very forgetful lately and Al wasn't much better. She picked them up, then realizing they were for the safe tucked snugly in the corner.

As she went to put them in a drawer, she suddenly pulled back, thinking I'm going to have a peak. Curiosity winning over honesty, she opened it and saw that their accounts and bills were in front. However, she saw a couple of big parchment envelopes in the back. Carefully removing them, she saw that they were tightly sealed, and each one had a blue ribbon around them. Against her better judgment, she put on the steam kettle on the nearby stove, then checking there no customers out front she put one of them into the steam braking the glue seam. She then carefully opened it, and what she saw completely surprised her.

It was the Will of Viola and Al, of a $1,000,000-dollar policy! Wow, Amy thought; my sister and the cops were right. It went on to say, in the case of death of either Al or Viola, or both; that their son Leo Rego, would receive $500,000, long time employee Mike Fremont $350,000, and Attorney Jack Cohen $50,000 for the work and dispersing the monies. When she continued reading, she saw Amy Rudy $100,000, and she almost fainted!

It took her a few minutes to regain her composer and take in a collective breath. Suddenly, she heard a customer and ran over quickly, selling the woman a gallon of milk. Within seconds she was back in the office. This time thoroughly scrutinizing the Will in detail, because she was so excited when she first read it that she failed to notice there was a double indemnity clause of accidental death. Then she tried to get her head around it, and realized the other envelope must be the standard Will. Then she remembered that Becky told her and Josh about the double indemnity, but she wasn't sure what she meant. Now however, it was clear; and if they die other than accidentally, or a death from a robbery or some other act of violence, probably must less was hers for the taking. Knowing she couldn't take a chance opening the second envelope, she very carefully re-glued the open one and placed them back in the safe.

Her mind was running wild. She couldn't believe they would give her that amount of money, probably less in natural death but who cares at this point, she was in disbelieve. Then, in regaining her composure, she went back to the front of the store.

Chapter 11

At home, Josh noted that Amy was always in a good mood. She was always humming some tune even though he was about to go on the unemployment ranks. He just couldn't put a finger on it, even sex was stepped up and frequent.

One day, Amy came out of the shower as the radio was blasting a J-lo song; wearing a leopard skin loin cloth and skimpy top. While Josh was on the computer, he noticed and his mouth dropped. "Hey, look at you! A wild Comanche Indian princess! Would you like to meet Josh; a nice guy cowboy that also has a wild side?"

"What's up baby?" she said as she sat on his lap.

Josh said, "Me now honey," then said "Wow, what's that sexy fragrance?"

"Its Black Opium do you like it?"

Josh licked his lips, "Do bears like honey?"

Amy gave him a sexy grin, "Remember when we first met and started dating and having sex at first? Do you remember what I asked you?"

Josh had a million-dollar smile. "How could I ever forget?"

"Well," she opened his shirt, rubbing his chest, "I want to hear it again."

Josh considered her sensual brown eyes, "You told me you and your old boyfriend slept together, but although it was OK, you were really never completely satisfied."

"Yes," Amy said.

Josh went on, "You weren't sure about every woman having a g-spot, that panacea of ultimate implosion; at least that's how you described it."

Amy grabbed his cock, feeling it struggling to push through the dungarees.

"And," Josh went on, "You told me, I got into you so deep that you..."

Amy cut him off, "You got into me with a *force,* that I felt wild gyrations, that I never fathomed."

She paused, as Josh gently picked up his little Indian princess, setting her down. As he dropped his pants his throbbing cock came flying out. She smiled and stroked it, "You remember how I climaxed three times? And that's no BS."

"Wow," Josh exclaimed, "Your words sounded like they came out of a romance novel."

Amy laughing said, "Well, I read them now and then."

Josh took his boots off, and slid off his dungarees, picking her up, and dropping her into the bed.

"Baby, do you want me to find, and rub that hidden spot?"

All Amy said was, "Do birds of the feather fly together?"

Chapter 12

Three months had passed, and Amy's memory kept unraveling. As it was around Christmas when she worked in the store, when River Cohen, Jack's stepson who was always coming in for something, came in that day, Amy sensed he came to see her.

"Hi Amy, just wanted to give you the great news! I passed the Bar!" Then he hesitated, "On my third time, thank God! My father wants me to join his firm."

"Hey, that's great River." "Of course, you know we never really got along, but my mother was on his back."

Of course, she never revealed that she couldn't stand his stepfather.

"So, you might call me a bonafide lawyer," he chuckled.

Then, thinking back more, Amy remembered a couple of months passed; into February as a cold rain mixed with snow permeated the area where Amy was working at Rodgers and Rodgers when the first bombshell hit: Attorney Jack Cohen died from a heart attack while playing Racket Ball. Followed by the second, bombshell: Al Rego died in a fall in his store. They were all over the papers and Facebook.

Then, around April, River kept coming in the store, and shooting the breeze, and trying not to seem that he was infatuated with her. Of course, she already knew that he was. Then, one day he told her that he's now handing the Rego Will. With that simple statement, a dark plot got into Amy's mind. Why? She wasn't quite sure. So, she had to see if she could manipulate River.

Then, yet on another River visit, she put on her charm in all her sexy allure. River fell like a junior high school boy, overwhelmed with his first look at a boob! As she was straightening up some shelves, she could see River ogling her body in a reflection from the glassware. She turned, "River, you got a girlfriend?"

River in a quiet reply said, "I had one, then she dropped me."

Amy walked over saying, "I don't know why."

As she looked into his eyes, she could see he was shy, as he kind of backed up. She knew that her plan must be done slow and carefully, and that means, not to reveal her true intentions; at least for a while. Then, Amy reflecting her memory-they had decided to go for a drive through Clarksville, further toward the Cape. Amy's intention was a drive, to where she and a few high school girlfriends went; to the lovers' lane on the edge of town. She told River to turn into a secluded road, then pull up between trees.

"Yeah, me and a couple of my girlfriends used to bring our boyfriends here. You know, the high school thing."

River then said, "You mean you had sex?"

"No silly, we'd just dry grind and drive them crazy."

Then she made her play, and was all over him.

River was in disbelief, and was breathing heavily.

"Relax." Amy quietly said, then locked her mouth to his.

Her tongue swirling and probing. River was all over her tits, trying to get them out of the bra.

"Wait River, we can do better than this. Do you know where the Anchor motel is just a little north of here on County Road?"

River thought, "Yes, I have seen it before."

"Okay, then can you meet me there; say Tuesday night at 7?"

Before he could answer, she followed up, "We will spend a couple of hours there. You game?"

River smiled, "I'll be there."

Amy now had her first leg on her plan.

Three months rolled on, and Amy was in an affair with River, the young lawyer. She was glad that he had no characteristics of his stepfather's surly attitudes.

Then one night, after she thought now that she could trust him; she said, "River a little while ago while you were fucking me with that magnificent cock of yours, you spit out I love you. Is that true?"

River was surprised at the question, and frankly embarrassed.

"Oh yes, Amy I do."

Amy sat up in bed curling her tongue around his nipple, "I am getting to be very fond of you, and not only because of your superior love making."

River then forced the words out, "I know your married, and I don't have a chance, but I can't help feeling that way."

Amy slid over in his arms, "Never say never."

Then she got up, and put on her short nighty she brought just for him, and sat at the small table fixing her face.

"You know River, I haven't been honest enough with

you. I've known about the Will for quite a while now. In fact, I've seen it."

River looked dumbfounded.

Finally, she went through how she found it, saying, "The Rego's son Leo gets $500,000, Mike Fremont $350,000, myself $100,000. All this since Al died. Of course, you only get $50,000 for the execution of the Will. Viola would be under her son's policy until she passes."

River knew that more was coming.

Amy continued, "I really think you should make more than that poultry sum. Wouldn't you think so too?"

Amy went back to the bed wrapping her arms around him.

"Maybe you can change some language and figures around. Maybe you can cut out Mike Fremont? That would free up $350,000."

River felt like he was being pushed into a box.

"Oh now, I couldn't do that. It's dangerous."

Amy released her arms, "Dangerous?! Are you kidding? Here in the motel, this is dangerous."

Amy made sure he knew she was clearly upset.

"I know what you're saying, but I know Leo knows about his $500,000, and of course Viola knows. I am sure she was privy to the Will, along with her husband, and Leo is the Executor."

Amy went from being upset, to being agitated. Amy licked her upper lip, "My thinking, is that without Leo knowing anything, you can say that Voila didn't want Mike on the Will anymore, and changed it to me. Then we can split it between us. For God's sake, everybody now knows Viola has the first stages of Alzheimer's."

"Well," River said, "People do change Will's, but it is rare. Also, it's rare that a Will would be changed suddenly, like by Mrs. Rego."

Amy emphatically reminded him, "You told me you love Jaguars, in fact, you and I could take a weekend in the mountains in the car."

River stiffed his face, "I don't know honey if this would fly."

"Cutting out Fremont," Amy pointed out, wouldn't be all that bad; if he doesn't find out. Besides he lives alone, and I hear he's got a juicy pension from the plumbers' union; he won't be poor at any rate." Amy then curled her mouth into a sinister comment, "I've come so far, and so close; why waste it on Mike Fremont?"

"I suppose, the owner of the Will… meaning Viola, *can* change the Beneficiary's; but she would have to override her son, and he's the Executor."

Amy had a look of gloom, saying, "I can see this is too complicated. Too many checks and balances."

River suddenly realized her despair might throw a wrench in his torturous love for her.

"Amy?" River suddenly remembered Ken Hall a disbarred lawyer. "I think I have a plan, but it's going to cost us plenty."

Amy's eyes brightened. "How much?"

"I'm not sure, but this guy knows people that for the right price, there's a way; and I am willing to bet he can pull it off."

"So," Amy inquired, "How do you know about him?"

"My father told me that he was caught, I think he said in Queens, New York; trying to milk a socialite out of some of her Will. He's got consulting business on the Cape in Orleans."

"So, my lover-boy, you think we might be in your Jaguar for a weekend of hiking, love making, hiking, and of course more love making?"

River got all flustered and excited just thinking about it. However, he knew he would have to grease Hall's palm big time to realize his obsession to be with her.

"Honey," he said, "I think my man can pull it off, but we've got to figure to out how much cash to give him."

"Hey," Amy was all ears, "I like an optimist."

Then she reached down grabbing his flaccid penis, that suddenly arched upward, "Oh my, you've got a big boy down there."

Chapter 13

Meanwhile, in Mount Granite, Josh was getting a little suspicious that Amy seemed to be going out too much. Too many appointments, she never picks up her cell phone, and even when she does, it's always static.

River left the motel right after Amy, a planned exit, never wanting to be seen together. On his way home, he got to thinking; the first time Leo talked to him and told him about the double indemnity clause was in a document prepared by his father a month before Al died. River suddenly became jumpy, oh my God, would Leo push his own father down the stairs? Then he got a darker chill. Amy saw the Will, could she have pushed Al down the stairs when he open the magenta door? No, no, not my beautiful Amy. She was clever and determined, but she would never go over the edge and murder poor Al!

Amy got home and found Josh uptight waiting for her. Josh gave a hostile look. "So, Amy, where have you been tonight?"

"Oh, one of the girls at work wanted to go for coffee; you know talk shop, but then because of girl troubles she canceled. Then, I remembered I left my make-up kit at the store; so, I figured I would get it. Why, is there a problem?"

"Really?" Josh didn't seem convinced. "Did you get the kit?"

"No." Amy ratcheted up her answer. "Stupid me, I should have known the store was closed."

Josh was going to say something further, when she cut him off.

"Then, I saw Doris; a customer, and we started shooting the breeze."

"Doris who?"

Amy looked surprised, "What's with the third degree? I never knew her last name."

Josh went to the reefer, grabbing a brew, "You seem to be going somewhere all the time. What's going on?"

Amy laughed. "Going on? The only thing going on, is it's been a long winter, and now it's the spring of April and I've been doing things now that it is warmer."

Josh eyed his stunning wife, standing there in a blue wrap around laced skirt and a sleeveless blouse that put a spot light on her over-all dazzle; for lack of a better word.

"Look, Amy," Josh began "I don't want to doubt you, but you know I worry about you when you're gone; guess you might say I'm insanely jealous."

Amy walked over throwing her arms around him. "Don't worry, my strong stone crushing husband; I assure you that your Amy will always belong to you."

Josh then got a little relieved, but thinking he's seen how men look at her trying to hide their stares when he was around; but what about when he's not there?

"Well, indulge me then, how about taking a ride with me to Home Depot to get a few things, and I'll check out that new mower I saw on sale."

Amy said in a sexy smile, "Rodger you, let me just fix my face."

"And," Josh conveyed, later we will stop at the Star Club you love. For some of their margaritas, and they've got ice cold draft German beer."

Chapter 14

Amy got word to River, by using the phone at Rodgers and Rodgers where she worked. To tell him not to meet at the motel for a while as Josh was questioning her whereabouts. She was paranoid that with all the technology now, that a cell could possibly leave a footprint so to speak to a link to River. At least for a while she would re frame from the conversations with him, telling him to lay low and meet at the store Sunday morning; but only if he could add more on her plan.

A couple of weeks later, after Viola got back from church and was doing what she could do to help Amy, and add up some bills to creditors, Mike Fremont dropped in unexpectedly. Amy was, at once in a stress mode.

"Ladies," he said as he walked in.

Viola looked up thinking she knew the man, but she couldn't remember him. Amy quickly said, "Viola, you remember Mike Fremont; he worked here."

Viola seemed confused. "Yes, I think so."

Amy winked at Mike, surely, he knows her deteriorating condition. Mike panned the area then commented, "I spent years helping Al and her, fixed many problems over the time, and I never asked for anything special. Just liked to help out."

Amy was trying to process his tone. Then he remarked pointing to a window. "Damn kids threw a rock through it a snow storm, but yours truly came to the rescue."

Amy smiled broadly, "That's great Mike, I know Viola and especially Al-God bless his soul were always grateful."

Mike scowled, "Those Lounge kids from over at Darnell Road, I would bet my bottom dollar they did it."

Mike walked over to the lighter fluid picking up a can, "Well I didn't come here to brighten my star, just needed the starting fluid."

After he left, Amy got a little bit apprehensive; almost like he knew something about the Will, but then again that's impossible. Besides, if he did, he would talk to River; now the man in charge. However, did he talk to River's father before his untimely demise?

River drove by the window hoping Amy spotted the Chevy Suburban pullout back, which she did. She told Viola she would be back in a jiffy.

Confronting him as he exited she said, "Good news darling, Hall is on board with our plan but he wants $75,000 for the job, $50,000 up front; the rest when the Will is final; meaning the payouts will be kept in escrow for 90 days until payment is realized."

Amy was at once in a chasm of despair raising her voice, "Where the hell are we going to get $75,000? This is crazy!"

River expecting her response, was ready, "Stay cool honey, I am going to take out a second mortgage on the office building." He then grinned wickedly, "I did what you wanted, for you to get $350,000"

"River, you shouldn't have."

"Don't worry, I want to keep our relationship intact, you know how I feel about you."

Amy had mixed feelings. On one hand, more money; on the other hand, continued affair with River, like most cheating throughout the ages, could end up them getting caught. Now, she realized the end must justify the means or it might be her poison.

"Don't worry River, I assure you, we can split it up anyhow you want."

Amy's mind suddenly felt fatigued. She bowed her head.

"Anything wrong baby?" River blurted out.

"I'm OK, just overwhelmed by your generous offer; but on the same token worried we might get caught."

She then clutched him. Then in a semblance of a sexy smile, she gave him a million-dollar hug; cementing it with, "Tuesday night at the Anchor?"

"I wouldn't miss it for the life of me."

Then, she told him how Mike Fremont dropped by and her concern.

"Don't work up a sweat about him, he knows nothing."

Chapter 15

Tuesday late afternoon came around. As Amy got out of work, she called Josh on her cell telling him she was thinking about volunteering. Helping the veterans out, and was going to the VA in Clarksville to inquire.

She already told River that they would rendezvous at the motel at 5 instead of 7, and she was hoping that Josh brought into it.

River stopped for gas on County Road just a little ahead of Amy. In fact, she didn't notice him getting gas, and all he could think was giving her a loving hug; after all he was in love with her, but when he looked up again, he saw the light blue Dodge Ram go by and he was sure it was Josh! Oh my God! He panicked, and he's following her! Afraid to call her, he remembered an adjoining road that he could catch up to her in a different direction. Then, realizing that she got too much of a start in front of him and Josh was right behind, he had to somehow prevent Josh from reaching the motel. Then, he remembered some orange cones that he saw on his last trip.

So, he put the petal to the metal; flying past Josh knowing he wouldn't know him from Adam. Then, he quickly switched the cones to reroute traffic to go around the construction site instead of through it. Then, at top speed, he reached the motel just as Amy was getting out of her car; he blurted Josh was coming!

Amy quickly headed for the VA, about 10 miles down the road. The whole time thinking it was too close of a shave, and she could see Josh bashing River to a bloody pulp if he saw them go in the motel together. She must somehow end the relationship with River as soon as he makes good on their plan. But how?

Amy pushed the old Chevy, and pulled in the VA parking lot and scrambled in toward the information desk, but before she did that she looked out the wide front window and looked across the apron of the parking lot and saw Josh's pickup slowly grabbing a slot in back. She quickly got in line behind three people, and after at least 35 minutes elapsed she got the info, and again she looked out the window and could see that the pickup was gone.

Thanking her lucky stars and then some, she headed home to Mount Granite. She also wondered, was it time or not to tell Josh about the money? She still didn't feel comfortable about this crooked lawyer.

Josh smiled as she walked in, "Hi honey, did you go to the VA?"

"Yup," she said as she went into the bathroom to brush her hair. "The information is in the packet I brought in."

"Oh, that's great." Josh was pleased. "Anything to do with the vets shows me you're a real trooper, but honesty I never knew you were considering volunteering. I guess I never knew your patriot side."

Amy laughed, "My mother once told me that a cousin in Ireland fought in World War I in France."

"Yeah, my dad was a Navy man; some people today, including some immigrants have no appreciation of the vets that have kept us safe from all who want to kill us. It seems that many think the country owes them a living."

"I know Josh, buts let's not get too political, you know I lean left on some things."

Josh didn't reply, just thinking he couldn't understand some of her views, and was better not to say anything.

"Josh, sit down, grab a cold one. I've got important… or I could say awesome news that will absolutely floor you."

"What?" he exclaimed, "Floor me?"

Then Josh broke open his Bud Light quipping, "I already know what your hiding from me. You're finally pregnant, and with twins!'"

Amy laughed, "No silly, good guess though, but your way off."

"Then what?" Overwhelmed with curiosity.

Amy had a million-dollar smile, "I found out yours truly, is in the Will of Viola and Al; and the payout if one them or both died. There is a double indemnity clause in case of an accidental death, you remember when Becky told us about that a while back? I will be receiving $350,000 dollars."

Josh felt he had lockjaw, "Are you serious Amy, who told you?"

"The lawyer handling the Will, in fact it's Jack Cohen's son, River."

"I never knew he had a son."

"Stepson actually," Amy answered, then walked to him, "I guess it pays to be nice to people."

Josh sauntered about the room, it was a huge surprise to say the least.

"You mean, you had no idea?"

"Not even remotely."

Josh, almost in a stutter, conveyed, "Now pretty girl, you can get all the things that I never could give you."

Amy corrected him, "Honey, material things are not that important as the love you have given me. Besides, were going to book a trip to a tropical island, on a private beach. Somewhere we can run around balky bare ass, and if we want make love as a wave comes over us."

Josh grinned, "Stop it, I'm already getting a hard on thinking about it."

Amy cracked up in laughter, "Yeah? Remember the last time on a beach what happened? We both got mega chafed from the sand."

"This time," Josh laughed, "We're going to find one of those small pools of water that mothers always play in with their tots, but for us we're not only going to screw until our hearts desire. Then, I am going to find your g - spot with my tongue; not only once, but 5 times."

"Oh Josh," Amy ran over in his arms, "I love you so much!"

Josh pointed out, "Well, I know one thing. Years ago, my Aunt Millie was left $200,000, and believe it or not, the IRS doesn't tax Wills."

"That's good news." Amy concurred.

"When's this all going down?" Josh asked.

"Soon babe, according to the lawyer."

Chapter 16

A week went by, and River rendezvous with Amy at the store. He told her that the parties, meaning her and Leo, along with Viola; were to meet at Jack's... now his office for the dispersing of the Will at 10am on May 4[th.]

Amy would be with Josh of course, and warned River to act cool., and, that there would be a notary present.

A few days before the target date, River was at the store and Amy had to keep telling him that the motel for now was out of the question. River grabbed her hand, "Amy I've fixed it big time on your payout and I don't want you to walk away from me like I was used."

At once, Amy recognized a red flag, "Of course not honey, why would you think that?" She then gave him a passionate kiss saying, "I get off in 20 minutes, but stay right here, I want you to park behind the storage shed, got it?"

"What for?" River was puzzled.

"You and I are going back to high school." she giggled.

In fewer than 15 minutes, Amy pulled up beside his SUV out of sight. Nobody ever goes out back she thought.

"Come on handsome, fold that back seat back; you and I are going to fuck."

River was beside himself, "Are you crazy? Here?"

"Don't worry, nobody's around. Just make sure you use a rubber like you always do."

River laughed, "I remember Cassie Ware from the ninth grade how, she got busted getting caught with Rodger Nelson in his T-bird behind a super market warehouse."

"Never mind that! Crawl in the back."

River was like a deprived soul, that his penis burned in carnal lust. His hands all over Amy's breasts trying to free them from the tight top and bra.

"Easy honey," she said as she pulled them out for his pleasures; and he quickly dropped his pants down enough to get his swollen cock out. Then, with both trying to accommodate movements to get into her, Amy cried, "Damn River, you keep everything but the kitchen sink in here!"

Finally, River moved sideways; sliding it in, and she murmured, "Yes, yes honey; it's in," but when Amy tried to get a better position it slid out, "Damn honey, it slid out."

"OK, OK let me move around some more." Then he got it in and all he said was, "Boy are you hot inside. My cock feels like it's on fire."

River didn't know if it was the adventure of the moment, or the chance someone would walk up to the vehicle, but it was only two or three minutes that he exploded into her.

He buried his head on her tits; mad at himself for pulling the trigger in a flash.

"It's OK River," Amy assured him, "It was the passion of the moment."

Then, they both disheveled; mangled to crawl back out.

Amy quipping, "Feel better stud master?"

"Yeah, sure," his face reddened, he looked down.

Again, Amy brushed it off and said firmly, "Let's blow this clambake, I'll see you on May 4."

Chapter 17

T he date finally arrived, and Amy put on a short skirt and matching blouse; glad that wearing pants in the winter and the cold spring, this year that finally the warmth of May was here. On the way to River's office in NorthPark with Josh, she was deep in thought; River fixed it so she would get the money that Fremont was supposed to have. Knowing now, that she was now super obligated to be in his debt; and that means continuing their illicit affair. She knew that winning him over had to include sex; then she laughed to herself, time tested from Cleopatra to Marilyn Monroe, however, the damn fool is hopelessly in love with me. She must pay him some of the money like he once suggested, but she gets the big chunk; and she knows that way he's getting to keep his little sex kitten. Oh my God! She became distressed. I think I really backed myself in a corner with no way out!

At a red light, as the sun was getting brighter; Josh reached over and put on his Oakley sunglasses and said, "You seem to be deep in thought."

"Just thinking hon," as she turned the radio on to an Adele tune, thinking, now things are going to be different;

now that we can pay off the mortgage, and I'll buy both of us new vehicles, and pay off those pesky credit cards.

Soon, after arriving at River's office, everybody exchanged pleasantries and poor Viola didn't really know what was happening; for as far as she thought she was invited for tea! Of course, Leo was now Viola's financial care taker; making sure that she had enough money for the rest of her life, and of course the eventual placement in a home that specializes in Alzheimer care.

So, with all said and done... the process went rather fast to say the least. Of course, when the big check was presented to Amy, both adulation and despair went hand-in-hand through her mind. River acted like he hardly knew her, and thank God kept his emotions intact from her insanely jealous husband.

Soon, they were headed to the bank of the check, where Amy quickly deposited it, then after an appointed time, they could withdraw it.

Amy said to Josh, "Well in a couple of days I'll be back at the store and who would've ever thought that the Rego's would leave me that amount of money.?"

Josh was still in semi shock, and commented, "Yeah, and you would have thought that Mike Fremont who worked there for years wouldn't have been included in the Will."

Amy adjusted her bra that was straining against her bosom, Josh tilted his head sideways where Amy recognized the same look when he decided to investigate the cellar where Al had fell.

"What's on your mind Josh?"

"Well, I don't know it just seems peculiar that Al and Viola didn't include him. After hearing that he was a Johnny on the spot for over ten years. Do you think he knows about the Will?"

"I doubt it," as Amy took a deep swallow of nervousness.

Josh sighed, "It just doesn't seem right at all."

Amy trying to keep her cool said, "I heard Viola changed it, but I don't have a clue why. Hey, my husband, look at it this way; he might have been Johnny on the spot, but Viola really loved me, I was always receptive to her wants and problems. Lots of people can't be bothered to lend their ears to elderly people, for its uselessly dull and uninteresting, and they walk away. My mom always told me to respect the ones before us, show them love and understanding, and cope with their different points of view; even if it's irrelevant of a different time. And above all, make them feel they still can contribute to the present moment."

"Hey," Josh said as he pulled out on the interstate, "I'm impressed with your spiel, but I can't help thinking, that if Fremont finds out, a tremendous anger would go to the depths of his soul. I am sure of it."

Into the light traffic, the Dodge Ram rolled along, as Amy added, "You know Josh, nobody knows this, but Al was somewhat abusive to her, and she told me that more than once he screamed at her, and on one occasion slapped her; and the only one she confided in was me."

Josh said, "Damn, who would have ever thought."

Amy digested the lie, and it made her feel better that it justified her over Mike Fremont, and hopefully Josh would think the same. Besides, what's one more lie, that seems to be in a quiver in her sack that she would use along with all the other ones?

Chapter 18

A month had passed, as Josh found it unusual that Amy never bothered to withdraw the money. Not even a penny, but kept mum about it. After all, it was hers, and he didn't want her to think he was frothing at the mouth waiting to help her spend it.

Amy was adamant about one thing though, a pair of smooth shiny shoes that she wanted for work. She told him she was going to check out the mall over in Clarksville and would wait for him when he got home from work, but on the cell, he told her he was too exhausted to go after lugging rocks around all day for the new library project at work. Amy` however, wasn't at the mall, but pulled into River's new cottage that he had built just to be alone with her.

River greeted her, "So what do you think?"

Amy got out of the old Chevy and looked around as the wind blew her hair from her shoulders.

"It looks cute from the outside."

River laughed, "A typical woman reply, step in I got it all fixed up."

Amy commented as she scanned the inside, "Boy, I guess you did."

River pointed to the kitchen set he just bought, then

showed her a jacked leather chair and love seat and a spacious leather couch covered in a New England Patriots cover. Amy was taken back on his taste for furniture, "Wow I didn't know you were a football fan."

River smiled, "Yeah most anybody in New England loves the Patriots."

The small getaway was only three rooms and a bath, but to River it was going to be their love nest; but before he could show her the bedroom she stopped him, "River we have to talk."

River looked a little rattled, and his light blue eyes seemed to flutter.

"Talk about what?"

"Sit down River," pointing to a chair.

River shrugged his shoulders, "Something wrong, my beautiful girl?"

"Yes, definitely." She was assertive, "I want to settle the money, I want to go with our first plan."

He could see that she was a little distressed, "Hold on babe," he chided "You're worrying for all the wrong reasons. Don't you remember, Hall gets $75,000 that I am going to give him out of my remortgage of my office. The $350,000 is basely yours, after maybe keeping a few bucks out in case of any unforeseen circumstances."

Amy suddenly felt like a fool, "It's not fair to you."

River snickered, "Don't worry about me, for the way I figure it, your worth more than any amount of dough."

"River darling, you keep forgetting that I'm married to a real maniac, and I am afraid that if he finds out you may end up on the bottom of Cape Cod Bay."

"That's why I built this secluded getaway."

River walked over to his new leather couch, feeling the material, "Have you ever got into bondage with Josh? They say it's a whole new experience."

Amy didn't appreciate the question, thinking their sex life shouldn't be brought up.

"Not good River, let's keep questions like that out of our relationship. I told you a long time ago not to compare our sex lives."

River was embarrassed, "Sorry Amy, I crossed over the line, and I should have known better."

Amy sauntered around the cottage checking out the quaintness and privacy, "Well, it's a nice place I must confess. Oh, by the way, Josh has been asking questions about why Mike Fremont has been cut out of the Will; sometimes he thinks he's James Bond."

"Well, just remind him that the payoff is far from being shabby, and for some reason, Viola left him out of the Will. Some say because of his gruffness. Being a braggart in her early stages of Alzheimer, if that makes sense, besides with Alzheimer I think we can run with it."

Amy sat on the love seat, of course River readily joined her saying, "This is nice, but the bed is nicer."

Amy knew that she owed him big time, and she felt better that the cottage was remote, and far less dangerous than the motel. She could see the familiar sexy grin in his demeanor, that he wanted her, saying, "Lock the door, let's check it out."

The room was well appointed, for a small living space. Its new bed had crisp sheets, and a western- style blanket.

Amy chucked, "The blanket has mountains of Montana all over it."

"Yup," River smiled "Were both going to have a great ride."

She grabbed him, starring in his eyes, "You're quite handsome you know."

He remained silent as her soft hand moved up, gently sliding across his cheek as he flashed a yielding grin placing his arm around her small waist, melting at her prowess. She gave him a great thank you hug for the money he forged for her, and now she truly wanted to make love, that in her mind would be worth all the $350,000 that was coming her way.

River could feel the bulge of his manhood rising to the occasion and she smiled kissing him, then they locked tongue's. Swirling, probing as the arising tantalizing concussion of the moment threw him back.

"Hey, you," River blurted out, "Did you take some jet fuel?"

"Relax," she whispered, her tongue lubricious, was in full command. With that, he slipped his hand up to her breasts, which strained against her tightly laced summer dress as she moaned. As he unfastens the lace from the six holes that held the bodice together, "Wait," she said; and let it fall on the shiny wooden floor, leaving her clad in a black bra that matched the always alluring thong; and although he has made love to her on several occasions, this time would be different. Special.

He momentarily froze seeing her strip off her bra and thong, as the sun shone in the window giving her a golden glow.

"River, get out of your clothes and lay on the bed face up. You and I are going to a 69 party at your new digs."

River was out of his duds in a flash, as Amy straddled him enabling him to work his way into her wet, tight, little pussy, and at the same time she sucked and sucked his burning cock as he was biting on his lip to hold in the eruption.

Amy was overwhelmed, as River got deeper and deeper into her, crying out, "River my God."

As she arched up to get more of his tongue that was curling and licking, giving her what felt like tiny little bursts in part of her that she didn't know existed; making her scream like she never did before, as River kept licking her even after she climaxed two times.

River didn't last more than a minute as Amy drained him dry. Amy was amazed at his prowess and told him so. Amy went into the bathroom to pull herself together, thinking that her boyfriend River is one glorious sexy man, she felt she gave it her all to settle her part of the debt. She further thought, although it may seem cold I must find a way to get rid of him.

Chapter 19

L ater that night, Amy came home as Josh was watching Jeopardy without a shirt. He looked up, "Did you find the shoes?"

"No; but not for lack of trying."

Josh got up, giving her peck on the cheek as she took in his steel body.

"I've got coffee on."

"Good" she responded.

Going into the kitchen, both took seats.

"Oh, your sister called earlier. I told her you went to the mall."

After watching the show Blue Bloods starring Tom Selleck, who reminded her of Josh when he was younger, Amy jumped in the shower and was totally surprised when Josh joined her grinning.

"I thought I would wash your back my love."

"Yeah, sure. The typical line that men have been using since probably Napoleon and Josephine."

He had a smile almost as big as his woody, "Are you saying that I am looking for your beautiful pussy?"

Amy laughed, "Your rabbit wants to go in the hole?"

After they finished washing, he dried her off. Picking

up all of 110 pounds, carrying her to the bed. Amy thought, my God my little pussy will be invaded for the second time today. Josh was like a panting dog, rocking back and forth in reckless abandonment; climaxing rather quickly, then apologizing for the rough sex. Amy put it aside saying, "Don't worry yourself, obviously you were super horny from the women that just seem to be around when you're working shirtless, sweat rolling down as you're picking up rocks."

"What are you talking about?"

"Honey, don't worry about it, they have to get through me to get to you."

"Amy you're crazy. What women?"

Then as he walked to the bathroom, he notated blood on his penis, alarmed he turned, "Are you ready to have that women thing?"

Amy voiced, "If you mean my period, not at all."

He walked back over, showing the blood on his penis.

"Oh, sometimes women can bleed just a little from a man who is rather large like yourself; and you were forceful enough; that's what probably happened."

Josh couldn't be sorrier, saying he was selfish in the intercourse not holding back, and felt more like a Roman Legionnaire subduing the women captives in his bedchamber and told her so. Again, he said, "Sorry honey, I didn't mean to be so rough."

Amy laughed, "It's OK big dick. Now go shower and quit watching all of those Roman Empire movies."

More than likely she thought, she did have two men, not that many hours apart. This though was something that scared her that she's becoming not only a whore for River, but acted like one to her husband, afraid to deny him or he might get suspicious. Then she thought maybe it was just a play of words, but although she got the money, she found herself feeling dirty; and that's something that she never felt in her whole life. Then another dark thought overtook her, how could I have been so stupid that I thought a few bangs with River he would go away. She wished she had never picked up those damn keys on the office floor!

Mike Fremont was no fool, when he found out that Amy was in the Will, and supposedly Viola took him off; that didn't pass the smell test and he flew in a rage. It was like a burn festering away, and he intended to find out more.

Chapter 20

A few days later, Amy sat at her desk at work in a tizzy thinking about what to do with River. Twice, her boss told her she was running behind on her sales report, and knew this whole thing was beginning to unravel. Thinking further, she had to talk to someone and the only one she could trust was her sister Becky.

The next day, a Saturday while Josh was doing some errands, Amy jumped in the in the shower seemingly trying to wash away her unfaithfulness and her lying and scheming that made her far from that cute seventeen-year-old high school cheerleader that Josh married.

She called Becky, and was glad she was home, and told her she had to talk about something important. She left Josh a note saying she was visiting Becky, and was glad for once it wasn't a lie.

Becky lived in West Dale, not far from Bensonville where she worked. Amy threw on a pair of shorts and a cute pink half belly shirt that highlighted her six pack abs that seemed appropriate for the warm weather. As she headed out with the Chevy's muffler really getting worse, she was thinking about how she was going to tell Josh in a couple of weeks they would start looking for new vehicles.

Becky was clad in a pair of cut offs, a tank top, and pumps waiting at the front door, and she could hear the music of Toby Keith coming from the house. Parked to the side was Pedro's brand new bright red Ford 350 flatbed 1 ton that he uses for odd jobs, and Becky told her that he keeps the shiny chrome duel rims so polished that she could almost do her makeup, and Amy thought of the song "Take It Easy" the mega hit by the Eagles.

"Hey little sister, I know you like iced coffee decaf, so I got some waiting for you."

"That's great," Amy said, as she admired Becky's Cape style home nestled in with well-kept neighborhood houses and well-groomed lawns.

Amy followed her in, where the AC was turning out a frosty relief from the heat.

"So," Becky said, "Can you believe this heat? Yesterday it was only 54."

Amy chuckled, "That's New England, just wait a minute, it will change, or something of that nature."

They both laughed when there was a rap on the door. Becky opened it saying, "Hi Reggie."

Amy could see a tall, young black man asking if he could borrow her lawn hose until he got a chance to replace his damaged one.

"Absolutely." Becky responded.

Then she came back and sat at the table, handing Amy the coffee.

"That was Reggie Demurs. The neighbors are so great around here, everybody has helped someone out at one time or another."

Amy smiled, "That's cool. Pedro on the road?"

"Yeah, he left for Pittsburgh yesterday; should be back tomorrow night. So, Amy girl, what's on your mind?"

Amy sipped her brew saying, "Beck, I'm in trouble."

Becky was taken back. "Honey, what have you gotten into? Is it about the Will?"

She nodded as she looked down, tears running, "That's part of it."

Becky joined her by the chair, giving her a hug, "Tell me more."

After Amy told her everything, Becky was shocked.

"Honey, you and River could go to jail for this. It could be grand larceny, probably falsifying documents, and fraud, and God knows what else."

Amy grabbed her sister's hand squeezing tight, "Oh Becky, what a terrible thing I've done. I got greedy stealing Mike Fremont's money, and using River for sex to get what I wanted. The list just goes on and on."

Becky thought about the moment and said, "Honey, let's be cool about this. Maybe there's a way out."

Amy looked up thoroughly distressed, tears running like a waterfall, "But, how Beck? River is insanely in love with me, and even if I were to give the money back, he wouldn't take it. Besides, he already told me, once it went down there would be no turning back."

Becky went to the fridge grabbing a Coke, "It's Josh that I am really worrying about, he would pulverize River beyond recognition with his Portuguese temper, and I don't want to scare you, even kill him!"

"No!" Amy blurted out, and then went into uncontrollable sobs.

"Amy," Becky raised her voice giving her a box of

tissues," Pull yourself together, now you told me that you think Fremont doesn't know anything?"

"Yes," Amy said drying her tears; "He doesn't; according to River."

"Well, a few nights ago," Becky began "Pedro's cousin, Lieutenant Gonzales told him that when they investigated Al Rego's accident, along with what I think he said Lighthouse Insurance out of New York, they opened up the Will to see who would benefit from an indemnity clause. Evidently, they could find no foul play so it was shuttered. However, a few cops saw the Will, and the beneficiary's including the Chief, so that leads to ask yourself could Fremont have found out?"

Amy now saw a noose that seemed to tighten around her neck saying, "Oh God I hope not! River says he doesn't know!"

Becky came back, "You know, River because he's crazy about you, probably never really thought of all the angles. All he cares about, is bringing you to the cottage you told me about, this love thing can be as deadly as a slug from a 38. Then there of course is this crooked Ken Hall, lawyer or not he'd probably dime you out if the heat was on to save his own ass."

Amy stood up, "I failed Josh. Even River, by including him in my stupid plan. I failed our extended family, our mom, and you, just to be a greedy asshole."

Becky turned up the AC a couple more notches, "Look sister, we need a plan; and if worst comes to worst, a good lawyer."

Chapter 21

Four days later, Becky's husband Pedro was told, and Becky called Amy and told her that he would do everything possible to help her, and wanted her to come over after she finished working at the store; and to keep her cool as he tries to dig up more. Amy agreed, then telling her that Leo is closing the store in a month, after almost fifty years because of his mother's apparent Alzheimer's.

When Amy arrived, Becky told her that Pedro's boss had called and he had to make a short run to Portland, Maine, but he has been considering what Fremont knows and he would do everything to help, and earlier today was sniffing around with some of his cop friends.

Meanwhile, Josh was wondering why Amy backed off her plans to withdraw the monies to buy the two vehicles they talked about, of course he didn't like asking questions, and kept silent.

River had been coming to the store for the last three weeks, and Amy kept making excuses, as to why not to go to the cottage, finally giving in, that she would meet him Tuesday night at five thirty.

After River left the store, Becky pulled in and went in. When she walked in she saw Viola sitting in a chair seemly oblivious to her predicament. Becky had a concerned look, and got right to the point, "Pedro found out that Mike knows about the Will," then she glanced at Viola.

"It's OK Becky, the poor woman is pretty bad now. In fact, her son was over last week to get ready to place her in a home, and like I mentioned before, he's closing in less than a month."

The salvo of what Becky said however, was now hitting her hard. Mumbling, Amy said, "He knows?"

"Mike also has a gun permit to carry, not that I am saying you're in danger, but for the last few times you're here, I am going to stay with you."

Amy gave her a hug.

"Don't worry little sister, I carry mace."

Chapter 22

Mike Fremont parked across the street from Attorney River Cohen's office, knowing, that River drove a black Suburban that was parked out front. Mike was liveried, that bastard had cut him out of what he heard was $350,000 but before he had a second thought, River exited his office and left.

Mike smacked his lips, thinking this better than he had hoped for. He now would wait less than an hour before it got dark, and with a pry bar, and screwdriver would break into the office to try to find any evidence that might shed a light on his suspicious thinking that River did something to change it.

He didn't see any cameras, but would have be careful of alarms.

Meanwhile, River stopped at a flower shop and purchased a dozen red roses on the way to the cottage, just counting the minutes before he laid eyes on his beautiful Amy, the love of his life that any extended time away from her was like a prison sentence.

On the way to the cottage, Amy felt like she was stranded in a bog of quicksand, slowly sinking and Josh on the bank watching her. She would plead, waving her arms for him to pull her out, but he would just look and laugh yelling, "Sink you whore, sink!" Then she shook it out of her reverie, and focused on a plan to get River out of her life.

River heard her muffler spewing car, and wondered why Amy hadn't bought a new one yet, Amy walked in to a display of roses, and a fancy card, as River was smiling like he hasn't seen her in a year.

"Hello River."

She then picked up the card reading it, "That's beautiful. You do love me, don't you?"

As she smelled the roses, he said, "Without question babe."

Amy instructed him, "Please sit down. Honey, my sister told me that Mike Fremont knows about the Will."

"What?!" River raised his voice, "I wonder how that got started?"

Amy said, "You know I really enjoy our encounters, but I have been getting a really bad feeling about this whole thing."

River was quick to say it was bullet proof.

"No, it's not! You really spelled out your feelings about me in the card, maybe if you love me that much we ought to find a way to end it."

"You can't be serious!" River began to unravel.

"Look," Amy said, "I haven't touched the money, and what if these rumors are saying, are true; I heard Mike packs a gun, and I also found out, which I never knew; he has a violent temper."

River suddenly was silent, deep in thought. Amy stared at him, finally saying, "What are you thinking about?"

River knew this was bad, if Mike knows. It was not a

death sentence though. Then he realized he was shaking, "I am sorry Amy," he managed to get the words out "I think we can get through this, maybe at one time he was on the Will, perhaps Viola changed it when Al died and my father never drew up the new papers, what do you think.?"

"No sport, don't you remember the time line? Your father died before Al."

River looked glum, "You're right, how could I forget that."

Then he went into the bathroom, rinsing his face with a cold facecloth looking over to Amy. "Don't worry hon, I'll figure something out."

Amy looked out the window, "Maybe we can somehow give the money to Mike, and it will go away?"

"Not that simple love, I am sure your husband would find out, and he's a big dude, and I would be toast."

Amy sat in the chair, consternation running rampant. River walked over, gently grabbing her hand leading her to the bedroom. She kind of hesitated, "River I don't think I'm in the mood."

He eyed her blue shorts, a skimpy almost see through top and sandals due to the obsessive heat wave gripping the area. He encircled her placing a passionate kiss on the lips saying, "Baby I always think a lot better after sex."

However, she wasn't ready to submit; but then thinking maybe he would get this Mike thing taken care of, even if I might have to fuck him until the cows come home! She sat on the bed and started to remove her top when he stopped her. "Wait honey, were going to something different this time; we're going to play strip poker."

Amy was startled, "Are you kidding? Strip poker!"

"Yeah, I thought it would be fun."

Amy, in trying to make sense of him, who just found out that the man who we robbed could be looking for us, wants to play sex games.

"Please River, why don't we put it on hold?"

"Oh, come on baby, let's just put this Mike thing out of our minds for a little while."

"Well, Amy scanned his attire, "Looks like your wearing more than me."

He laughed, "It's all in the cards Amy, and the rules are, whoever loses goes down on the winner."

Amy broke out in a tirade of laughter.

"What's so funny?" He looked puzzled.

"I can't believe you! Although, I must admit, I needed that laugh."

"Well, baby," staring and resplendent of her scanty covered body hoping he loses this one he said, "Hey, it's funny because it's going to be fun."

He picked up the deck of cards, saying low card peels of an article of clothing. "You go first sexy woman."

Amy got a five, and he got a nine and she kicked off one of her sandals; next pick she got a three and River a jack, "Hey, your cheater. This game is rigged!" came Amy's sassy conclusion as she kicked the other one off. The next round, Amy beat River, queen to eight and River removed a shoe.

Before long, she was down to her shorts and thong, but then she made a comeback and River was down to his boxers. The next turn was Amy three, River six.

He was feasting on her perky breasts and admiring the marvel of her near perfect form, but when she dropped her shorts, his manhood crashed against his gray boxers as he zeroed in on her red thong thinking he'd like to rush her and pull it down.

"Wow," he said, "You're a beautiful woman Amy."

Then on the next cut Amy drew a jack but to his overwhelming delight he drew a ten.

"How about that?" he said.

Amy smiled, twisting her hand, saying, "Off with the boxers."

Then with no further words spoken between them, he gently slid off the thong. Although he has more than once had oral sex with her, he knew that every time would be better than the last time. Amy was like a shiny jewel that the more you rubbed it the shinier it got.

River went down on her, licking her covet sanctuary with such a delightful zeal that compressed feelings unraveled her whole body into a chamber of feel good spasms.

"Oh, River," came from her lips.

He couldn't hear her as he twisted and licked his tongue, then finally, then and only then he had to bring his throbbing cock into her. Amy could only wonder what suddenly fused all her bliss into uncontrollable passion deep inside her, as River raked her with a new barbarism; pushing any gentle stokes to the wayside. She was spitting out broken words as River brought her once again to finality that caused her to scream in raw passion.

Finally, after a blistering fifteen minutes, they both were well spent. Amy thought, my God what a rush! River studied her face, and it looked like she was shy in expressing such a moment, that he asked, "Honey, do you love me?"

"River babe, I really want to, but I am afraid that I don't know what could be coming around the next corner.

Something good or nonferrous, but I must say you're more of a man than I realized."

That set him off to kiss her breasts and whispering in her ear "Remember the song Nine to Five by Dolly Pardon? Well hon, no hours for us for with the money, and my practice we will be able to vacation at will."

"You're forgetting one thing lover boy, my husband the Paul Bunyan of Mount Granite."

River shook his head "Honey you shot down my wishful thinking."

"It's called reality," she bristled.

"I know, I know," he concluded as he got dressed, "I am going to do some homework on this whole debacle."

Then he departed the cottage.

Chapter 23

As Amy drove home still thinking about River's erotic love making, she thought how it didn't sink her plan to end this husband-boyfriend nightmare. She saw that Becky had sent her a text, so she would call her later, but now she had to deal with Josh. At the cottage, she had taken a long shower, then locking up for River; as he wanted to get to his office in a hurry.

Thankfully, Josh was working overtime on a wall in Bensonville, and she knew that he was probably wondering why she hasn't touched the money yet so she did what a nice little wifey does; make supper for her hubby. However, the thought sent her to the bathroom in a sob, thinking like in the Roman Empire books that Josh is always reading, infidelity would probability mean a severe flogging or worse.

River drove to his office, and at once noticed right away something was a rye when it looked like the side door was jimmied. When he walked in he knew for certain Mike Fremont knows about the Will, and because his step father was so cheap he never installed any alarms.

Amy rustled up some pasta and beans, and made one of his favorite deserts Johnny Cake. She also made sure there was plenty of beer on ice. Herself, all she felt like eating was a cold bowl of corn flakes, then snapped on the TV and the news.

The weather man was saying the obsessive heat would continue for one more day. "Thank God," she said out loud.

The next morning, Amy left for work and was glad that Josh was so exhausted that he fell in a deep sleep and never got frisky; then in response to Becky's text that she came over after work to talk to Pedro.

Earlier that day she buried her evil thoughts about River by paying someone to eliminate him, it just wasn't her. She pulled into Becky's driveway in West Dale. She conferred mostly with Pedro, an immigrant whose father brought him over from Mexico when he was a boy. She could see the real concern across his face about her dilemma, but he couldn't really offer any real solutions except not to run into Mike Fremont. Amy drinking her iced coffee quipped, "Pedro, what exactly have the cops been saying?"

Pedro, semi dark skinned, barrel chested and a little taller than her, got up from the table and went into the panty to lite a cigarette.

"Amy, the cops only know that he was told, supposedly by Leo at one time about the Will, but he has a temper that the cops know about when he was arrested for DUI several years ago."

"Any more news about the store?" Becky asked.

"Just that Leo is looking for a buyer."

Then Pedro said. "If I were you, I would say, how do you say it? Watch your back when you're with the lawyer."

Chapter 24

T wo months passed, and Amy withdrew some monies paying off the mortgage, and bought herself a Chevy Tahoe SUV, and Josh a Chrysler 300. She sold the old Chevy Impala to Josh's friend Carlo Perry for a first car for his son who was attending a vocational school to revamp it. Already he and his friends at the school had restored a bright yellow 87' Oldsmobile Cutlass Supreme. Josh kept the Ram in case they needed to haul anything.

About a week later, in another cottage encounter, River told her how Mike must have ransacked his office probably looking for a duplicate of the Will, but he's got it stashed away at his mother's house; and then he told her of the plan he came up with.

If Mike further took it up with the cops, or the insurance company, he would say that soon after Al died Viola came to him knowing that he was in charge handling the Will, for it was no longer Cohen and Son but River Cohen Attorney of Law. She had him dismiss Mike and put in Amy in for the $350,000. She also instructed him divide up the $100,000 that Amy was originally going to get, to the other parties; of-course he was wondering why she would do that but it's none of his business. Then they, meaning Light House Insurance and Causality would investigate, of course finding out that Viola now has Alzheimer's big time. Both River and Amy now seemed a little more at ease, for there was neither hide or hair of the handyman and plumber Mike Fremont.

Amy and River continued their elicited affair at the cottage, Amy now always buying something new for her husband to keep him in a way occupied; for her always going on phony mall trips. Josh wouldn't care, she was just spending her new-found wealth.

One Saturday afternoon, after she heard him come out of the shower, she stopped him.

"Baby, stay naked and get in bed."

Josh's eyes lit up. "Wow, this is a treat. It's only five thirty."

She cupped his balls saying, "This, is an afternoon delight. I'll be right in."

Josh jumped in the bed surprised his sexy wife was overly assertive, then he laughed thinking his grandfather would say she's feeling her oats! As he lay there under the sheet, she came in with a small, plastic sack; suddenly dumping its contents on the bed.

"What's this?" He said, looking at dildos.

"My girlfriend at work has been educating me on the art of dildo doing your husband."

Josh sat up, "What are you out of your mind?"

"Relax honey, she said you would likely act the same way her husband did when she first suggested it."

Josh was beside himself, "Amy you're plum crazy if you think you're going to do that!"

"Come on my big boy, give it a chance."

"No chance! That's not natural."

"Honey, I have three dildos; all comparably small, and a vibrator. She told me what to do, and believe me, this is only to pleasure you."

"Amy, your ass is made to get rid of stuff, not to stick things in."

"Not only has my girlfriend been telling me this, but also I picked an instruction booklet at the sex store. Now, pull the sheet off dear; I've got a couple of pillows for you lay on."

"No," he just laid there with his arms folded.

"Josh, honey," Amy put her body next to him, "Now please. Don't be so stubborn, you know I wouldn't do anything to hurt you."

"Honey," he said, "That's the gays thing."

Amy laughed, "Well I assure you, you're not gay husband."

"Ha, ha very funny."

"Look, tonight I'm only going to use the smallest dildo; for you to get used to it, then in the next two or three weeks the dildos get a little, let's say wider, until they're the same as the vibrator."

"Amy, I love you, you know that so get your clothes off and let me give you a heavy drilling. Now wouldn't you like that?"

"Oh baby, that will happen soon, for when your ramming me, the self-propelled vibrator will be going up and down in your butt."

"What? No way!"

"Now, my Tarzan!" she said as ripped the sheet off forcing him to turn over.

All Josh did was crack up laughing, "Ah, that's more like it, big baby."

She, for the first time realized his ass was part of the sexual component that had been missing in their love making; for he's always calling her breasts and rump as well as what he calls her tight little pussy beautiful things, of course she always loved to call his big dick a thing of wonder, but now she found herself mesmerized and eager to insert the dildo up his ass.

"Don't worry baby, I got plenty of K-gel."

As she slowly pushed the dildo into him she found herself getting excited and sweaty.

"Easy," he called out.

"I'm doing it gentle my rock crusher."

After about a half hour and only a few complaints, Amy knew that Josh had passed the first test. The real clincher came when he stood up, his cock seemed longer and wider than ever before, that she wasted little time in taking as much as she could get in her throat, and mad sucked him that in less than a minute he came off; and for the first time she didn't pull away swallowing it.

"Amy, damn that's the first time you did that!"

"Rewards benefit you being a sport champ." as she went into the bathroom.

Chapter 25

About a week later, Josh joined Amy who was in the cellar working out; sweat running down her face.

"Hey, look at you; no wonder you got a dynamite body."

She smiled, keeping her pace on the treadmill.

"No different than you champ."

He laughed, then said, "A while back, I noticed a slight crack on one of the pipes going to the water heater to the boiler," then he investigated further, "Yup, I'm going to put this on a short bucket list."

Amy, now lifting small weights, looked over, "How bad is it Josh?"

"Don't worry about it honey, I'll take care of it."

About a week later, Josh was on his lunch break and drove over to the West Dale Mickey D's about a mile from where he's helping his boss do some patching of an existing wall. After driving through the drive in and sitting in his new Chrysler, he thought he noticed the man coming out of the front door as Al and Viola's part time worker Mike. However, he had only saw him once and wasn't sure. He watched as the man reached in his pocket to retrieve a napkin to wipe his hands then chucked it into the rubbish container, and Josh noted a card fell on the ground. He decided to walk over to quell his curiosity, picking up the card, it read: Mike Fremont; Plumber, Good Rates. On it were two numbers, shop, and home, but no e-mail. Josh thought, hey this is great, I was looking for a plumber to replace the pipe in the cellar. Before he left, he went in to use the rest room, and on the way out two cute twenty or so girls looked up, one saying, "Didn't we see you building a wall across from Wal-Mart?" then the other girl kind of giggling said, "Why don't you join us? We want to know how to place those slabs like you do."

Josh laughed, and said, "I would ladies, but both of you have got such pretty fingernails that I would feel bad if you broke one." Then as hard as it was he had to brake his lustful look at their awesome bodies, with breasts teetering, ready to spill out of their colorful tops.

Amy was home before him, sitting in living room chair as he walked in, and said, "Hey baby, you look like you've got a convict's headache."

"What's that mean?"

"It means someone who is bored."

"Oh, I'm not bored, just thinking about what to make for supper. What about dropped eggs on toast?"

"Sound like a plan, pretty lady."

"So, how was your day?" She inquired.

"Not bad."

Then he told her about seeing Mike Fremont, and how he got his card. Amy at once was in a panic mode, saying, "Oh no Josh, I've heard stories about him; that he does shabby work."

Josh was surprised at the strong rebuttal, "Well, I

thought that you guys used to work together at the store, maybe we would get a cut on the price."

Amy looked kind of disheveled, her face red, "No Josh, customers told me he's a rip off."

"OK babe, I'll get someone else."

The anguish suddenly began to deflate from her mind.

"I'm sure you can find someone else in the area."

Chapter 26

Amy, on her way to work one morning thought a car was following her. At work, she kind of dismissed it and went to her computer.

A couple days later, as fall became on the chilly side, her sister called her at home telling her that the doctor prescribed her some news pills for her supposedly constant headaches. After telling Becky that things were quiet, that she and River for the most part were keeping low, Becky said be careful; that might mean a bad omen.

Amy got a little rattled at first, but dismissed it; but then thinking, poor Becky all her life she and her best friend Julie have been popping pills and now Julie is in a clinic in Concord, New Hampshire. She prays that sometime Beck will get off those damn pills, thinking that in the long run, they can be deadly, especially now with the opioid crisis.

Amy glanced at her watch, she was to meet River at the getaway in a couple of hours; knowing that for now she must keep him happy, for who knows what he would do if she broke it off. Although she loved Josh, she must play pretend with River. As Amy headed to meet River, Josh was on the way home after picking up a chain for his chain saw, when in a back yard he saw what looked like an old 54' Ford slowing down. He thought that would make an awesome street rod.

River and Amy rendezvoused at the cottage. River had a million-dollar smile, knowing once again he would be under the sheets with his cutie doll.

At the same time, back at Amy and Josh's, Josh went down cellar to check on the leak.

"Shit!" he exclaimed.

The leak was really getting worse, and even though Amy was against calling Mike, he thought he would take a chance because of the gravity of the situation, but couldn't remember where he placed the card.

"Damn," he muttered. "Where is it?"

So, he needed to call Amy, although she doesn't want to do business with him, but finding a plumber can be hard in Mount Granite. The two he knew of retired. Perhaps she saw the card.

Meanwhile, River was admiring her new SUV when the phone rang and River asked, "Who is it?"

"It's Josh, but I told him I was going to the mall so he probably figures with all the noise that I didn't hear it or that it wasn't on vibrate."

"Will he text you?" River questioned.

"Not a chance, he doesn't text."

River walked over to the new Chevy Tahoe, looking in the window, "Nice ride, but black's hard to keep clean."

At that moment, Mike Fremont came around from the back of the house pointing a gun.

"Well, well, the two love birds; my lucky day!"

River turned white, and Amy's heart sank.

"Now both of you are coming with me."

River managed to get the words out, "What's going on? Why the gun?"

Mike now seemed furious, "Shut the fuck up, asshole. Turn around, put your hands behind you."

River knew the gun was a 45 automatic, and it looked like Mike was becoming unhinged. Quickly, River and Amy's hands were tied, with tie cords and they were further restrained by having duct tape across their mouths. He then forced them in the back seat of the older Ford F-150 double cab to lay down. Then he pulled out saying, "I've been following both of you for weeks, nice little gig you got. River stealing my money, and fucking a man's wife. Well boys and girls, I got some R&R scheduled for both of you, and I am sure you will enjoy it; in fact, Elvis has left the cottage permanently!" Then he let out a blood curling laugh as he headed to NorthPark towards his shop.

Meanwhile, Josh had decided to drive to his old home town, remembering there were NorthPark exchangers, although, he didn't remember a plumbing shop, but he had moved out several years ago. Mike Fremont pulled into his plumbing shop's back driveway, in what once was a farm and the shop a converted slaughter house; parking behind the old high walled building kept him out of view from the only neighbor in the area. Pointing the gun, they were pushed and pulled out. Amy tried to bolt, when Mike smashed her across the mouth. She hit the ground hard, knocking one of her earrings off.

"Nice try slut, you better save your energy for what I've got planned for you."

Then waving his gun, he marched them into his office,

then without saying anything, he strapped Amy into a metal chair.

"This ought to keep you."

Then he violently shoved River to a different part of the building, on the opposite end where they once slaughtered livestock. After a brutal walk, where he whacked River with a rubber hose, then threw him down on the cement floor, he said, "River, where's my money? The $350,000 you forged to give to your slut?"

Then as River tried to get up, Mike ripped the tape from his mouth repeating, "My money asshole! Or has the bitch already spent most of it, and if she has you two are going to pay dearly. She didn't buy that SUV on chump change."

River exclaimed, "You're crazy! It was left to her in a Will drawn up by my father!"

Mike struck River on the side of the head with the rubber hose, "You're a fuckin liar, you slimy lawyer. Now one more time sunny boy; where's the money?"

River pleaded, "Please don't kill me. All I know is Viola changed the Will after Al died, and I put it together; and that's the truth."

Mike snarled bring down the chain fall, "You're going to wish you were never born you piece of scum."

First, he cut River's binds, putting his feet upward in the chain fall, then securing his hands. River screamed and cried, "What are you going to do? Please don't hurt me!"

Mike took his penis out, pissing on his face saying, "I want the whole story. From A to Z. NOW!"

River tried to bluff his way out, "Mike, Viola got Alzheimer's, that's why I think she changed the Will."

"No, that's a crock of shit. You changed it to impress the whore."

"No Mike, no."

Mike picked up a box cutter, making quick work of his clothes. River hung like a piece of meat screaming and pleading for Mike not to hurt him.

Mike smiled, "Oh, I'm going to hurt you. Big time."

As he picked up a blow torch from a nearby bench, he said "Where's the money cocksucker?"

River howled when he saw him light it.

"Again. The money asshole, or you're going to have roasted balls."

Chapter 27

Josh arrived in NorthPark, and stopped at the fire station, and at once recognized Jess Ryder whom he graduated with.

"Hey Josh."

The firefighter extended his hand, "Long time no see."

"Yeah, it's been a while. You ever see the old gang?"

"Matter of fact, I ran into Tom Jensen the other day. He works for a real estate broker over in Bensonville, and I asked him the same thing, and he told me that the Andresen brothers moved out to the Midwest somewhere, and Billy Tinkham, you must remember him; he's a buyer for some department store."

Josh said, "Oh I remember him alright, I ran into him several years ago in a coffee shop, and he acted like his shit don't stink. What a complete jerk. One day, I ran into Hilly. We didn't go to school together, but downed many a drink at the old Rock House lounge."

"Yeah, I remember him," Jess said then added, "What about your old best friend Dave Mason?"

"Yeah, Dave and I get together now and then, and we talk on the phone; a matter of fact he ran into Bobby

Nickerson a few weeks ago, and I would put him in the same category as Tinkham."

"What about big tits Nancy Chernard?" Jess laughed.

Josh smiling answered, "I used to call her a stacked brat in the eighth grade and she loved it, but I have no idea what happened to her. Probably married somewhere with five kids."

"So, my friend, don't tell me your looking for directions?"

"Yes, a matter of fact I am, looking for a plumber named Mike Fremont, he's got a shop here in NorthPark."

Jess rubbed his chin, "Never heard of him."

Then he hesitated, "Heard someone opened a shop at the old Smith field farm. You must remember that place they used to slaughter livestock around World War 1. That might be him. Remember it was on the edge of town on Shagbark road?"

Josh said, "I remember, a big old thing, that the kids used to call Frankenstein Castle."

"Oh, by the way, I like your driver. A Chrysler 300, that must have some balls?"

"Yeah," Josh said, "It's fast, but I was originally going to get a Dodge Challenger. They got a Hellcat out now, but Amy talked me out of it saying every young kid would be wanting to race me; and she knows my temper, I would probably kill myself."

With that Josh bid farewell and headed for Shagbark road.

Chapter 28

Amy struggled against the blinders, knowing her cell was only inches in her front pocket, but might as well be a mile away. Then thought she heard faint screams, due to thickness of the walls. She flayed, and struggled against the tight blinders, knowing she had to get free to get to her cell.

"Oh my God!" she yelled, as she heard what sounded like more blood curdling screams. He must be killing River, she anguished.

Mike walked in as she struggled to escape, "Forget it whore! Your piece of shit boyfriend told me everything. That you were behind the plot all along with that fuckface lawyer Ken Hall, whom I'll get later, maybe a little accident."

Then he burst out in a roar, "Boy, those inquisitors were right to say the truth is through pain."

He walked around her, "All the time, I thought he was the one in charge of ripping me off, but it was you that got my $350,000, pretty clever huh? With that money, I was planning to send my two grandchildren to college and I was going to buy myself a Mercedes, then drive buy my no-good ex-wife smiling and blowing the horn. But you, you fucken cunt, wanted it all. Sucked River's dick to get everything that was mine"

Amy could see that Mike was having a melt-down.

"You're fucking dead boyfriend tried to lie his way out at first, but I just pin pricked him with the blow torch so he wouldn't become delirious; just small burns to keep him talking, then after he confessed everything I started to enjoy myself burning his nipples off. Boy did he scream, then I burned his skin all over. Burning, blistering, and bubbling torturing him, but then it got messy as he lost his bowels so I put a bullet through his head."

All Amy could do was cry, and sob through the duct tape, knowing he was going to kill her. Suddenly he ripped the tape off her face, laced with a death sheen then cut the binds.

"Now stand up cunt, it's time for you to be the big star tonight."

Then he threw two ropes over an overhead beam and tied her hands upward, then secured her ankles to the Lally Posts.

"Yeah baby, this is your debut. I've got something special for you."

Amy tried to master the words in a shattered voice, "Mike, please I've got a rich aunt in Newport, Rhode Island that will give you money. Just let me go, that's all I ask."

Mike slapped his hand across the corner of her mouth drawing blood, "Nice try, liar." Then he went over dragging over an old cobwebbed mirror.

"Oh," he laughed, "You're going to have a front seat to your own miserable death."

"No!" Amy screamed, "Please don't kill me!"

Mike grinned, "I'm going to kill you alright, that's after I torture you first. So, put on your dancing shoes baby you're going to have a star-studded performance."

Then Mike walked away for a moment, then came back over carrying a small metal bin in his hands putting it near her face and shaking it sarcastically he voiced, "Gee whiz, Amy what could this be?" showing her the tiny metal bits inside. "What you don't know, is this is one of your props for your Hollywood extravaganza, so all the audience will be cheering you on. You see my pretty, I'm going to hang you upside down, your legs nice and wide then I'm going to dump these in your cunt, and take a stick and push them down; so, feel free to scream so the crowd can have a good show. Remember, you're at the Mike Fremont studio, so lass give them a good buck for their money."

Amy screamed, "You're sick, you're sick!"

"You're right, but before we do that, I am going shave all the hair off your body, starting with your head, and eyebrows, and especially where River enjoyed so much. So, shall we get started?"

Amy screamed again, as he pulled off her sneakers and tore off her shirt, and cut off her pants and underwear.

"Ach," he exclaimed, "Well toned, strong. You must work out, and that's good. You will take longer to die bitch," and then gave that blood curling laugh. Then, bringing over the scissors and electric razor he shaved her head completely bald. In the mirror, she looked in horror as he shaved off her eye brows. Then he said, "This is my favorite part."

Crouching down, he made quick work of the hair on her vagina.

"Oh, you look good. My Hollywood starlet, but before

we start the show, I'm going over to the pot belly stove to grab a coffee, so you just relax while the audience takes in your nude hairless body; all toned up ready for the show of your life."

Chapter 29

J osh pulled up in front of the old shop as the sun started to go down, but noticed a pickup partly obscured. He walked over, seeing a Ford F-150, then remembered he saw Mike get into it at McDonald's. Good, he thought; he must be here.

Mike walked over to Amy, "You look radiant Amy girl, even hairless. But, as much as you want to flaunt yourself in front of the crowd and the world-wide TV audience, you know of course they want me to fill up your naughty snatch. However, there's a couple of preliminary things I must do to you, and I am sure you won't mind, and will get you in the mood to scream. All it means, is I am going to snip off your nipples, and run a wire brush up and down and twist it up your anus."

Then, he hung her by her ankles like he did River, with her head a couple of feet off the ground. Walking over, he picked up the bin, heavy with small bits and shards of metal. He showed it to the imaginary audience.

"See what's going to happen to this whore who ripped me off."

Suddenly Mike heard boos. "What the hell are they booing about?" Then the people started laughing and joking saying, "What a stupid old man, that he got ripped off, by a now hairless pussy."

"What! That slut fucked me over," but the audience just pointed their thumbs down and someone yelled save her pussy!

Mike, in shock said, "You're wrong, she's going to die slowly."

"No, no," the people began to chant, "Save Amy's pussy, save Amy's pussy!"

"You're crazy, you Hollywood elites, you are fucking glass house morons, she's going to die!" Mike screamed, but the audience kept chanting, "No, no, her pussy is up for an Oscar, don't harm her!"

Others kept yelling, "Save Amy's pussy!"

Then, suddenly some of the crowd, and all the Hollywood reporters converged around Amy, still bellowing "Save Amy's pussy! Get away, you sorry old man!"

Mike tried to push them back, but they shone their cell phone lights in her face while others snapped pictures of every part of her tormented nude body for Facebook, while still others reached down with their cell phones in her vagina streaming to social media yelling, "An Oscar for Amy's pussy!"

Josh noted a refection from the waning sunlight, near Mike's truck. Walking over, he picked up an earring, and was shocked that it was Amy's. He was sure of it, he bought them for her. Then a tremendous uneasy feeling overtook him, why would Amy's earring be here? I know it must be hers because I got them from the Navaho Indian nation, hand-made topaz.

Josh then walked past the huge high walled monstrosity

toward the office at the other end of the building. When he looked up to one of the few high small windows and was immediately startled by what looked like a silhouette of a person hanging upside down in the mix of darkness and sunshine at this exact point defecting a macabre image. Walking further down, he saw what looks like a rusty crowbar leaning against an oil drum, and grabbing it tightly he was beginning to feel a dark fear as he got closer to the office and thought he heard an awful scream, and quickly called 911 giving his location and concern, and he ran to the old wide wooden door.

Mike Fremont, now a vengeful monster, was sharpening his scissors to snip off Amy's nipples.

"There's the star of Fremont productions, Miss Amy," as he waved the scissors, "Are you ready to scream real loud now? Don't forget, the final curtain call is when I fill up your pussy, so control yourself for being so happy!"

Through a crack in the dilapidated door, Josh looked in horror seeing Amy hanging upside down. Then in a Herculaneum feat of strength, he ripped off part of the old rotted door with the crowbar. He rushed in, as a startled Mike went for his gun. In a split-second, Josh whacked him with the bar shattering his arm, and he ran for the door; which was suddenly covered with cops with their guns out.

Two of the cops helped Josh lower Amy, while another wrapped her in a blanket as she was spent of everything possible the human mind can process. She was shaking uncontrollably, but her eyes were starring out in a blank look of a twisted ordeal that traumatized her. She never even said a word, like she didn't know him.

The NorthPark police Chief told Josh that the medics

were on the way. Soon, the whole grotesque picture became clear; a young lawyer River Cohen, was brutality tortured and murdered. Josh's wife Amy, was almost the killers next victim. Of-course, now the cops knew nothing of why.

In a few weeks, Fremont confessed everything. Blaming through his lawyer, that he had temporary insanity, and killed River in a rage because both he and Amy stole his $350,000 along with disbarred lawyer Ken Hall.

Although Amy was saved from a grizzly death, she was already his next victim by having to be admitted to a psychiatric hospital in Bensonville.

Chapter 30

Almost a year had passed, and Josh every week would visit his Amy at the Claymore Healthcare facility, where they had an intensive state of the latest medical advances in her kind of trauma. Although, the chief medical doctor had told him that she could possibly come out of it, there were no guarantees; as he would spend hours talking to her as she lay there still, almost lifeless starring at the ceiling.

He almost had to give up the house, until a distant cousin Cam Phillips who was looking for a place agreed to move in and pay some of the costs, as he was recently divorced from his wife Diane so it was a good fit. The insurance company tried to attach the house to recover the monies from the fraudulent payout, but so far, his lawyer had beaten back the challenge, but told him to still pay the mortgage and put it in a fund because of the uncertainly.

Josh had to sell both the Chevy Tahoe and the Chrysler 300 and was only left with the trusty Dodge Ram. HE kept going over all the lies that she perpetrated on him, half was disappointment and anger, while the other half was contrite and forgiving, and deep down he knew what he always knew; he was deeply in love with her. He kept thinking that maybe her motive was to seduce River to get the money, then find a way to end it, maybe he was wrong with that kind of reasoning, but he would stay at her side forever if necessary.

It was a Saturday morning, when Josh got up and made breakfast; thinking back to when Amy in her PJ's would call him in and tell him that the coffee was on and he would join her, watching her bounce around the kitchen; joking and bubbly, that sometimes she never stopped being that cute teenager that he fell in love with.

He glanced over to the credenza, to where the pair of Navaho topaz earrings were, and thought how he found one on the ground that probably saved her life.

At that moment, the phone rang. It was Chief Williams, and he wanted him to come down to the station in NorthPark. Josh was surprised at the call and wondered what could be next. As he drove to NorthPark thinking that his poor wife, no matter what she has done--including being unfaithful, she has already paid big time by that pervert and sick motherfucker of a plumber by having all her body hair shaved and having to be tortured in a disgusting way was beyond the pale. If the cops didn't come in time, he would have killed him himself.

Soon, he pulled into the police station and was at once in the Chief's office, as Chief Eric Williams, a 55-year-old black man, told him to take a seat and asked how his wife was doing. Josh kind of looked down, "I'm afraid it's going take some time, according to the doctors. But, I always pray for a miracle."

"My prayers are with you," the Chief concurred.

"The reason I called today, two therapists from the

hospital where Mrs. Viola Rego is, told me some interesting information that it seems out of the blue. Mrs. Rego confessed to pushing her husband down the cellar stairs when he opened what she called the magenta door. Now, in our investigation of the death of her husband Al, we found no evidence, other than accidental, and the only thing I gleaned about the door, was someone painted it magenta and the wall at the bottom was also magenta."

Josh quickly filled him in about the story of the previous owners of the store, and that their kids painted it years ago. Josh then said, "Boy, that's wild. Her pushing her husband down the stairs."

"Well," the Chief reiterated, "Of course, with her Alzheimer's it's not too unbelievable."

"But why?" Josh couldn't seem to wrap his mind around it.

The Chief came around from behind his desk saying, "The therapist's told me because of his cheapness in never buying her any clothes or anything."

"That seems unlikely she would do that over something as trivial as clothes and things." Josh responded.

"I agree," the Chief was quick to say, "But, who knows; maybe the onset of Alzheimer's was in its early stages, and it wouldn't take much of a frail woman as Mrs. Rego to push him from behind. However, I don't think we will ever know for certain, but I know Amy worked for her, and thought you should know."

"Thanks Chief, it's certainly a mouthful to swallow."

Soon, Josh was once again on his way to visit his wife. As cold wind came from the Northeast, he was praying Amy could beat the odds. The Dodge Ram steady rolled on, and Josh wondered if Viola really pushed her husband down the stairs as soon as he opened the magenta door?

Who knows in a sometimes unforgiving world.

Printed in the United States
By Bookmasters